Praise for
DON'T TAKE THIS THE WRONG WAY

"The stories in Kim Magowan and Michelle Ross's collection are sharp-toothed, playful, trippy introspections on the mundane insanity of office-life, the gluey-soup of dating, the casual cruelty of childhood. This collection explores the grimy underbelly of what it means to be human—raw and honest, real and revelatory. Each story is a geode waiting to be cracked open. We couldn't say it better than the very first story in the collection: 'Enjoy! It's a command.'"

—DANA DIEHL & MELISSA GOODRICH,
authors of THE CLASSROOM

"Kim Magowan and Michelle Ross have created a smart and hilarious masterpiece of a collection. If you want to laugh out loud, this is the book to read; every sentence is a delight. Two heads are absolutely better than one if those heads are Ross and Magowan's. *Don't Take This the Wrong Way* is insanely good in every possible way."

—LOUISE MARBURG, author of
YOU HAVE REACHED YOUR DESTINATION

"How lucky we are to have this new collection from Kim Magowan and Michelle Ross, two of our best writers of short-form fiction. These stories are resonant and layered, nuanced and generous, each one packing a novel's worth of insight and wisdom and gifting us with glimpses into the rich interior lives of their characters. Building these stories together, Ross and Magowan have written us a wonder!"

—CHRISSY KOLAYA, author of CHARMED PARTICLES

"Writing stories has never been an exact science, but what a formula these two authors have used to create this perfect chemistry, an ideal compound synthesized from their individual elements. Magowan and Ross lend their unique voices and perspectives to make *Don't Take This the Wrong Way*, an amalgamation of the highest order, a wondrous and tragic and hysterical collection that employs each writer's vision, resulting in something new, something considerable. Two of today's best short story writers have collaborated to create one of the story collections of the year."

—**MICHAEL CZYZNIEJEWSKI, author of**
THE AMNESIAC IN THE MAZE

"Each story in *Don't Take This the Wrong Way* strikes like an elegant weapon, quick and sharp enough to take your breath away. The flash stories are masterclasses in the genre, showcasing the authors' talent for achieving precision without sacrificing complexity, and the longer stories are delightfully inventive. A triumph from beginning to end, these are stories whose impact far exceeds their length."

—**GWEN KIRBY, author of *SHIT CASSANDRA SAW***

DONT TAKE THIS THE WRONG WAY

Kim Magowan
& Michelle Ross

EASTOVER
PRESS

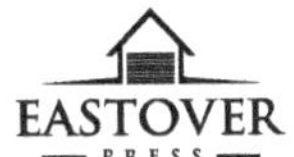

DON'T TAKE THIS THE WRONG WAY

Short Stories

ISBN: 978-1-958094-56-3

EastOver Press encourages the use of our publications
in educational settings. For questions about educational discounts,
contact us online: www.EastOverPress.com or info@EastOverPress.com.

Book Design by Beste M. Doğan

10 9 8 7 6 5 4 3 2 1

Published in the United States of America by

EASTOVER PRESS
Rochester, Massachusetts
www.EastOverPress.com

CONTENTS

DONT
TAKE
THIS
THE
WRONG
WAY

KINDNESS WOMAN

KINDNESS WOMAN HAS BEEN WORKING here barely seven months and already we hate her. This hate is of a different flavor than the antagonism we feel for Faye, who takes so many damn smoke breaks over the course of a day that even her emails reek of cigarettes—emails that often include full sentences in all caps, sentences that bend and break with her scorn like the cigarette stubs she twists and grinds into a tin coffee can behind the building.

Kindness Woman's brand of obnoxiousness sits on the opposite end of the spectrum as Faye's. Her emails contain rainbows—each sentence a different color and font. Her emails invite us to help ourselves to the cake or brownies or homemade cranberry-walnut-unicorn bread baked for our enjoyment on this beautiful day. Her emails always end with the word, "Enjoy!" It's a command.

As if that isn't enough, some days she will walk around the building hawking a platter of brownies or a jar of lollipops. She stops at every desk. She says, "A brownie to make your morning sweet?" or "A lollipop to brighten your afternoon?" The price: only your dignity and having to endure her self-satisfied grin.

Kindness Woman won't just anonymously leave her baked goods in the kitchen, like everyone else around here who wants to kill us slowly with sugar. Kindness Woman wants credit for her kindnesses. She wants a standing ovation.

"The thing about her is she never matured from high school," says Terry, who works in HR and maintains that HR will turn the sweetest, most extroverted person into a misanthrope, so it's not her fault she hates the world. "She's still on the hunt for Senior Superlatives. Cheeriest Demeanor! Most Spirited!"

"Most Likely to Fill Up Your Email With Exclamation Points," I say. Terry and I exchange a meaningful glance. Exclamation points are to us the splinters of punctuation marks. We share a deep disdain for those rows and rows of exclamation points in Kindness Woman's emails, stiff and spiky like the barbed hooks of a stickaburr. We share a disdain for enthusiasm. Sometimes the only words Terry and I will exchange over the course of the day are "Shoot me now." And yet—and I am being completely sincere here—we communicate so much with those three words, depending on where emphasis is laid. "Shoot *me* now" means seriously, it's my turn to moan. "Shoot me *now*" conveys urgency, that this level of bullshit is surpassingly dire.

Now Terry says these words, and she emphasizes all three.

Her emphasis is so extreme, it brings to mind Kindness Woman's exclamation points, but I don't point this out to Terry. Kindness Woman is the reason for this bloated, bloodshot "Shoot me now." Because Kindness Woman filed a complaint to HR against Faye for being mean to her.

"There's a form for meanness complaints?" I say.

Terry squints at me. "And who do you think Pamela tasked with the joyous assignment of investigating this complaint?"

"What's an investigation entail exactly? Do you tap their phones?"

Because we're talking in the break room, we both eye the door constantly.

"Why doesn't anyone file a complaint against Chad?" is what Terry says.

"Hard to prove a man is consciously looking at your breasts every time he talks to you?" I say. "Could be like being cross-eyed? He could say he can't control his eyes?"

Terry pulls her earlobe. "For starters, I have to talk to these women. I have to sit down at a table and have conversations with the two most intolerable women in this lunatic asylum of an office. I have to get their sides of the story. I have to take the complaint seriously."

"Don't take this the wrong way, but I'm kind of envious. I want to be a fly on the wall. Maybe you could record your interviews? Just surreptitiously turn your phone face down? I'd love to hear Faye explain why she's mean to Kindness Woman. What do you predict? 'Because she's fucking annoying?'"

Terry does not crack a smile. She folds her arms over her chest and looks at me bleakly. "Do you know why I got into HR?" she says. "I thought I could do some good in the world. I thought I could have some kind of influence on, say, diversity of hires. On practices of inclusivity. Bringing in good people and, okay, slapping the bad people, because dudes like Chad deserve to have their lives made uncomfortable. But no one utters a peep about Chad! Instead, I get complaints along the lines of, 'Faye said, Get those blondies out of my face, I do not give a shit if they have butterscotch chips.'" Terry bites her lip, then passes her hand across my forehead. "Obliviate. You didn't hear me say that."

Terry is always doing this, letting confidential things slip and then wiping my memory clean. I let my tongue hang out and glaze my eyes in response, performing successful memory eradication, but there is no cheering Terry up today.

"I think I've finally hit bottom," she says. "I think this is the bottom of the goddamn well. The ninth circle of hell, here I am, getting chewed on by fucking Satan."

"Here's what I don't get," I say. "Isn't this against Kindness Woman's whole ethos? Isn't lodging an official complaint pretty much the antithesis of kind?"

Terry looks at me pityingly. She says, "Isn't our company

motto, 'All for one, and one for all'? Yet you remember how Pamela said to Julie when she found Julie using Isaac's office when Isaac was on vacation, 'You're not on an office-level paygrade.' And then Julie came to me about it, me in my little cubicle five feet outside of Pamela's office! All I could do was laugh until my face hurt. I said to her, 'Julie, when the president of the company is also the director of HR, and your complaint is about said president, what do you expect me, who is also not office-level paygrade, to do about it?'"

Pamela enters the breakroom then, so I quickly switch the subject. I say, "Yeah, I started buying the generic sparkling waters. They taste the same, but they're nearly half the price."

"Which flavor?" Terry says.

We try to look like we're not monitoring Pamela out of the corners of our eyes as she slices a chunk of Kindness Woman's latest will-you-please-be-my-friend bribe: something crumbly and weirdly white, like it might just be made entirely of sugar. That or cocaine.

"Lemon," I say, "though the coconut is pretty good, too."

Normally, I take pride in my ability to quickly come up with inane shit to talk about in Pamela's presence, but right now, for some reason, I feel this sickening sadness. A lost-every-tooth-in-your-mouth kind of sadness. And that's when I remember that I had this weird dream last night that I was excruciatingly depressed. Weird because normally I dream out-of-this-world shit, but a dream about being depressed is dreadfully of-this-world. In the dream, I was walking very slowly through a putty-colored landscape. I was on my way to buy Cascade liquid-powder combination dishwashing capsules; my shoulders were slumped. When I first woke, it wasn't immediately clear to me that I had been dreaming, or was now conscious, or what, if anything, distinguished the two states. I actually said out loud, "Wait, what?" and rolled over to my left. But of course, there was no Karl lying next to me.

"Anything wrong, Grace?" Pamela says. She's watching me narrowly with her bulbous eyes.

"I was just remembering this incredibly boring dream I had."

"Hmm. People say they have interesting dreams, and when they describe them, they're incredibly boring. I wonder if that would make a description of an incredibly boring dream interesting? Or would it just be that much more boring?"

Pamela's affect is so flat and deadpan that it's impossible to distinguish between her philosophical observations and her jokes. Terry takes a gamble and laughs, and Pamela smiles graciously, so we know Terry guessed right.

"Well, I'll leave you two to your dreams and sparkling water," Pamela says, and departs holding aloft her powdery square of Kindness pastry.

Terry raises her eyebrows. "Now I know how to get Pamela to make a fucking fast exit. That was even speedier than when

Sam starts telling stories about the latest accomplishments of her twins." She looks at me more closely. "Hey, what's up with you? You look like someone hit you with a hammer."

There are a lot of things I could say at this point, but what I latch onto is what I woke up thinking, what made me so sad my reflection in the bathroom mirror shimmered and blurred. "I miss Karl."

Terry looks at me, just looks at me, then nods. I'm pretty sure I know what Terry's thinking but not saying—that I was the one who pushed for the separation, that I said Karl lacked the introspection to really love someone.

We hadn't yet separated when Kindness Woman first showed up, and I told Karl about that woman's damn emails and her peddling her treats around the office, and he said, "You sound like that Faye woman. It's like you're allergic to kindness. It's like you want to be miserable." I tried to explain to Karl: it's not kindness if you're constantly begging for credit for your actions and if you're pissed off when people don't give you the thanks you believe you've earned. I said, "Maybe she believes she's being kind, but that's not kindness. It's phoniness." I'd talked before that point about us separating. I'd already said many times that I didn't believe he really loved me. I'd said to him that I believed he believed he loved me, but that I didn't feel genuinely loved because I was constantly having to ask him to be thoughtful towards me, and on the rare occasions he was thoughtful, he made a big fuss about wanting me to praise him. When I called Kindness Woman phony and manipulative, that was the turning point for Karl. That's when he said, "You know what? I think you're right. We should separate. Because you're impossible to please."

That's when I thought, shit, he really doesn't love me.

"Shoot *me* now," I say.

Terry—who passed me Kleenex six months ago and said, "But Grace, isn't the point that you didn't really love him either?"—nods again, turns her fingers into a gun, and takes aim. I'm standing there waiting for that too-slow, invisible bullet to pierce my heart when Kindness Woman enters the kitchen. She looks at me. She looks at Terry. Then she turns around and leaves, as though she couldn't remember what it was she'd wanted.

PICKING

I'M PICKING LEMONS FROM THE LEMON tree beside the back porch of a man I met a week ago at a fundraiser for the local cat shelter. Cocktails and Cats. I was mostly there for the cocktails; Josh was mostly there for his ex-wife, Maggie. She's one of the shelter's directors. "She's my best friend," he said at the bar, and I nodded as though this were perfectly normal.

How about you come over and help me make a lemon cream pie, he texted when I said yes to getting together.

I wondered if lemon cream pie was a euphemism. I texted, *I don't like lemony desserts.* He texted, *but you haven't tried my lemon cream pie,* not exactly settling the euphemism question.

This is my first date since my divorce, which was amicable, but I wouldn't call Danny my friend. He's more like a security blanket—tattered, threadbare, embarrassing really, yet hard to give up. I'm on a mission to stop missing Danny, and I hope Josh, a confident man who sends decisive texts conveying concrete plans, can help me do that. Because now here I am picking lemons and inside the house, there's a pie pan and flour on the kitchen counter. (Turns out lemon cream pie means lemon cream pie.) Making homemade lemon cream pie is about as un-Danny as it gets. My ex couldn't even manage simple nachos. Always by the time he pulled them out of the oven, the chips were scorched.

This lemon tree is pressed against a chain-link fence dividing Josh's backyard from his neighbor's backyard. Two limbs fringed with yellow teardrops reach out over that fence like the come-hither gesture of a noir femme fatale. The people in that yard, a tatted-up woman in an orange one-piece swimsuit and three fully clothed women and an assortment of toddlers, pay the lemons no mind. The woman in the swimsuit minds everything else, though. She's a frantic bundle of energy careening around the overgrown yard. She reaches into the tall grass and plucks out a human child, places him onto a wheat-colored blanket where he is more easily visible. She inspects a stubby row of three tomato plants shaded by a small child's plastic slide. She picks up an unattached garden hose, moves it to the other side of the plastic kiddie pool that none of the children are using, for which none of the children are even dressed. The water in that pool is a strange milky hue, like glue.

"I call that the mosquito nursery," Josh whispers.

One of the toddlers puts a fistful of dirt into her mouth. The three clothed women sit quietly in fold-out chairs, as motionless as mannequins. I envision a photo shoot: The gritty suburban.

Maybe the shoot would be for an article about race in America. The sitting women are white, all three plump. The busy, swimsuited woman is Asian American. I'm pretty certain the only flesh on her body that's pinchable is her small breasts.

In the house, this strange backyard scene is visible again from Josh's kitchen window, and now that we can talk at ease I say, "Is that a play date?"

Josh piles the lemons into a colander and rinses them in the sink. "There are parents and toddlers streaming in and out of that yard all day, every day."

"But they all look so uncomfortable."

Josh hands me a grater and a lemon and tells me to grate.

It's one of those graters that looks like a metal spatula. From the concave side, the holes are perfectly round, but from the convex side, the side for grating, they are three-dimensional teardrops.

When I was in the last stages of my marriage, something strange happened to my vision: it became extremely sharp. I would look at random appliances, things I saw and handled regularly, and see all these new-to-me details, such as those contoured teardrops on the grater. It was like I was viewing objects through a times-ten microscope. My friend Elodie was pregnant at the time and obsessed with her suddenly acute sense of smell. We'd speculate about the evolutionary purpose, this ability to smell dog pee on the sidewalk from twenty feet away. What poisons were pregnant women protecting their fetuses from? I finally told her about my super-vision—I'm not sure why I was keeping it a secret, but I hadn't told anyone, even Danny. Frankly, it scared the crap out of me. I was afraid I had one of those brain tumors that turned people into geniuses or clairvoyants. Elodie, sounding like the psychotherapist I used to see in graduate school, said, "Why at this particular moment in your life do you think you need to see everything really clearly?"

The super-vision dominoed into a cleaning frenzy, but not a particularly satisfying cleaning frenzy in which one moves toward a final domino that will smack the floor, signaling the end. When you can see as well as I could then, you're never satisfied; you never relax. Everything is grimy. Watching the swim-suited woman go, go, go around that overgrown yard, I wonder if she suffers a similar extrasensory glitch.

"Is she always in motion like this?" I say.

Josh says, "She drives Maggie insane, too. The Mosquito Nanny, Maggie calls her."

My hands stop grating. Insane? Maggie?

"I only asked a question. You think I'm being driven insane?"

"Sorry," Josh says. "Maggie—" Then he says, "I should really stop talking about Maggie. She warned me about this. She's—" He holds up his hands, which are covered in sticky globs of buttered flour.

Back in the bar, when Josh said his ex-wife was the director of the cat shelter, I'd looked around, trying to decide who was Maggie. I thought she might be this languid woman with straight black eyebrows who looked like a sorceress. But then Josh pointed her out. Sawdust-colored hair that, were it a paint swatch, would be named "Nondescript." A turquoise felt ball dangled from each of her ears. They looked like tiny cat toys, and the way they swung about when she turned her head, I imagined tiny cats perched on her shoulders, batting at her earlobes. I narrowed my eyes, wishing I still had my super-vision so I could see what was secretly captivating about her.

What's really whacked is that the real reason I went to the cat shelter fundraiser was I'd been hoping to run into Danny. Every Christmas, he writes a $50 check to that shelter. Danny adores cats, but he's allergic to them. His eyes turn red within minutes of sharing air with a feline. He jokes sometimes that being allergic to cats is the great tragedy of his life. I used to think this was funny, but after a while, I thought, no dude, the great tragedy of your life is that you've never got any new material. Danny is like paper that has been recycled too many times, its fibers too short and weak to hold together anymore.

But there I was, hoping to see him anyway. What badly constructed object did that make me?

I ask, "Why does she call your neighbor 'The Mosquito Nanny'?"

Josh looks a little startled, then wipes off his buttery hands. "That wading pool, they leave standing water in it. We were always concerned it was a hazard."

I register "We." Maggie's still all over him, a filmy residue.

He says, "Also, Merguez—she's the woman in the swimsuit—"

"'Merguez' like the sausage?"

He nods. "Hey, have you ever been to that Tunisian place on McAllister with the amazing merguez?" When I shake my head, he says, "Anyway, Merguez the woman, not the sausage, has a tattoo of a mosquito." With his elbow, he turns on the faucet to rinse his hands. He dries them, then daintily taps his chest, his fingers still greasy looking. "Right above her nipple."

"And the answer to the natural follow-up question?" I say.

Josh grins. Points to a window in the house opposite, where a small, red four-legged figurine sits. Is it a horse? A dog maybe? A year ago, with my super-vision, I would have been able to see its eyeballs; now I can't even identify what kind of creature it is.

"Merguez's bathroom," he says. "She never pulls down that blind."

"Still, I don't see how you could see from this far. Is the mosquito the size of a fist? Mosquito on steroids?"

Josh pulls open a drawer. Between a stack of tea towels and a box of plastic wrap are binoculars. "Don't look at me. I swear I've never used them, not even when Maggie told me I *had* to see that mosquito."

"Does Maggie still live here?"

I never was any good at dating, so it figures the first guy I meet after Danny would be in some weird purgatory with his ex. I look around the kitchen for more evidence of her.

"What? Of course not. Actually, I do know a guy who lived with his ex-wife for six whole months after they divorced. Because that's how long they had left on their lease, and they could barely pay that lease on two incomes as it was, so a second lease wasn't an option. It was a one-bedroom too and neither wanted to sleep on the couch for six months, so one week the bedroom was hers, the next week it was his."

I'm about to comment on how perverse this arrangement is, when I think, wait, why do I care about two random strangers? Everything with Josh is a deflection. So I ask the question I've been avoiding all week. "Why did you guys split up?"

He grimaces. "Why did you and what's-his-name get a divorce?" That's how little I've talked about Danny, compared to Josh going on and on about Maggie: he doesn't even know Danny's name.

Or do I mean how little Josh has actually listened to me?

I scrape the wet lemon rind from the grater. Josh watches me, then says, "Maggie is really honest. Like, pathologically honest. I used to wonder if she was on the spectrum. She has no awareness of social niceties. You know, someone will ask, 'Do I look OK?' and she'll say, 'Good thing OK is all you're going for.'"

"'Someone' meaning you?"

People generally choose partners at their aesthetic level, or if there is an imbalance, it's the woman who is more attractive. I read some article purporting to list the thirteen characteristics of happy couples, and one of the characteristics was that in heterosexual pairings, the woman should be more attractive than the man. Apparently, both the man and woman are happier when she's the more beautiful of the two: he thinks he scored, and she feels desirable. But Josh is way better looking than Maggie. Whenever I meet a mismatched couple, I carefully study the uglier person, especially when the uglier person is female, to figure out what they bring to the table. It seems bizarre that Josh would need reassurance, or that Maggie could respond to such a question with anything other than a grateful, "yes."

"Actually, I was thinking of her friend Colette, who was so, so insecure. Colette would regularly leave our house in tears. 'I'm just being honest,' Maggie'd say. She didn't get it at all. Believe me, it's not easy to live with someone who feels like she needs to comment on one's every—" he grimaces—"performance. She had no filter. If she'd kept her thoughts to herself, different story."

Different story, as in Maggie would be the one wrestling with this grater?

I scrape more lemon goop into the bowl, considering. Unlike Maggie, I did keep thoughts to myself. One such thought occurred when Danny and I were at a restaurant, and I ordered a bowl of potato leek soup. The soup wasn't bad, but it wasn't good either. I tabulated its qualities (warm, not hot; bland, not flavorful; a little mealy), and then I had a thought: Danny is like this bowl of soup. The thought was so awful, and so boomingly loud in my brain, I pictured it exploding like a huge, pink gum bubble all over our table. But, of course, my revelation wasn't audible, though it expanded and kept expanding in my head for the next few weeks, until it was the bass hum to every other thought, and I'd think it while watching Danny peel off his smelly (but not truly odiferous) socks with my unbearably sharp eyes.

Since our divorce, however, I wonder if that acute vision hadn't been quite what it seemed. Not a brain tumor, but also not keen insight. I knew this guy in college who had a photographic memory. Pete was a B/C student, but not because he was lazy. The way he explained it: the mind can only store so much data, so when his brain memorized useless information such as the pattern of a random stranger's freckles or the buttons on their blouse, that meant there was less storage space for the useful stuff. Maybe scrutinizing Danny up close had been akin to gorging on the wrong information. Maybe that's why I'd had a revelation about Danny as a bowl of soup: my subconscious was trying to tell me I'd hit saturation point.

Who doesn't look a little ugly if you zoom in too close? I think of the magnifying mirror in Danny's mother's bathroom. I'd go in there thinking I looked good, but if I glanced for too long while I washed my hands, all I saw were pores like craters.

Josh puts his hand on my shoulder, and says, "Watch." I look up and see Merguez has just entered her bathroom.

Maybe Danny's best qualities are visible only at a distance. Like the tattoo above Merguez's nipple. I watch her in her bathroom as she pulls down her orange swimsuit, exposing her nipples and the tattoo. From where I am, I don't see a blood-sucking, stick-legged mosquito. I see a beautiful, feathery fishing lure. I see the flume between Merguez's nose and upper lip, her architectural collarbone, and her eyes, catching mine, widening in what appears to be recognition.

OH-OH-IT'S-CRUEL

WHEN MY SON FRETS OVER THE LIGHTNING bugs his cousin has trapped in a plastic bin that used to hold individually wrapped biscotti, my brother Shane says in his son's defense, "I don't give a flying fuck about insects." Then he says, "I think a lot of people care more about animals than they do people. They're all oh-oh-it's-cruel-to-eat-animals, but meanwhile, do they care about the homeless guy sitting on the street corner? Do they care about their own family?"

We're here at Dad's house for the weekend to be educated about his and our stepmom Gillian's will. Dad wanted us to "know in advance what's what so there won't be any arguing" after he and Gillian are dead and gone. I laughed when I read that in his email. He sent me a separate email asking if I would agree to be executor of the will. When he announced that detail this morning, my brother Shane blurted, "But I'm the oldest!" My sister Lorna and my stepbrother Mike said nothing, but their bodies visibly stiffened, making me think of royal icing when you let it sit for too long and it dries and forms a wrinkly skin.

My husband Grant is inside helping Dad and Gillian hook up their outdoor stereo speakers while the rest of us sit on the back deck, drinking mojitos—all of us except Lorna, who's in AA and made a big fuss earlier about how she couldn't miss the local chapter meeting this afternoon. Our drinking mojitos means we have to put up with Lorna's cigarette smoke without a word of complaint or else she'll launch into a mumbled soliloquy about how all her life we've conspired against her.

———

"Oh, like I want to do this," Carrie says. "Like I'm jumping up and down to be the executor of his will. Do you realize what a pain in the ass this will be?"

Mike nods in his sedated, bobblehead way. Everything moves slowly with that guy. Being stoned for ten years straight has thickened all his reflexes. He's a human mashed potato. But Lorna looks at me, cigarette clenched between her fingers, and her look is as legible as if she passed a note. We both know Carrie.

When we were kids, Carrie was a dictator. She sucked on grievances like they were jawbreakers. When we played Monopoly, Carrie insisted on being the banker, because she claimed I once stole $500 from the bank. She would hold up the game to make sure that exactly a third of the house purchase money went each time into Free Parking: $67 precisely, Carrie thumbing out the bills while Lorna and I moaned and groaned. She's anal as hell, which my parents always mistook for responsibility.

I remember Mom giving her a bag of potato chips to divvy out. Once Mom got sick, she was always sending us out to the lawn with various snacks. "Go have a picnic," Mom would say, so she could nap. Not only did Carrie deal those chips as if they were cards, making sure that Lorna, me, and her got the exact same number, but also, she decided that one of my potato chips was too large, and gave Lorna a bite of it to make it even. "Just this much, Lorna," she said, tapping the potato chip.

When Mom was alive, she called Carrie "My little hammer," because of the way Carrie would go apeshit playing Whac-A-Mole. There are people who venerate fairness because they have an authentic sense of justice, and then there are people, like Carrie, for whom fairness is an excuse to cudgel everyone into submission.

—

"I call your bluff," Shane says, and I'm transported to high school when I complained to Gillian and Dad that it was sexist to always put me in charge of watching Lorna and Mike when they went out to dinner alone. They'd say, "It's because we trust you. We wouldn't trust Shane to keep a fern alive through the evening." Then as soon as they left the house, Shane would say, "You're not fooling me with your cries of unfairness. You eat that shit up."

Shane's kid Lenny already has more lightning bugs in that container than one can count, but still he's running around the yard looking for more. He reminds me so much of Shane. Greedy as hell. He won't stop until he captures every damn lightning bug that makes the mistake of crossing the property line. And his demented glee when he captures one! "Don't even think about getting away!" he yells at the insects as he scoops them out of the air, floating flakes of gold.

My son Robert is in full-blown distress. He's got a chunk of hair wrapped around his finger, and he's tugging like he's trying to unearth a stubborn turnip. If Grant catches him, he'll launch into another lecture about how Robert's going to develop a bald spot like I did as a kid. Grant isn't particularly fond of Shane, but when he's irritated by my stressing over something, sometimes he'll say that my brother's coolness is admirable in a certain way. "Like how a psychopath's lack of empathy for his murder victims is admirable?" I say.

"And what the hell is that supposed to mean, Steve McQueen?" Carrie says. "'I call your bluff': are we gamblers? Are we in some bad Western? Because if so, get me out of this shitty movie."

In the backyard my son, Lenny, zooms around pretending to be a velociraptor, his arms extended wings. Lenny tries to get Carrie's son Robert to play with him, but Robert is a crumpled-up hedgehog in the hammock. He keeps pulling his own hair, a weirdo like his mom. "Baldy," I used to call Carrie.

"It means if you think being the executor is such a drag, then politely decline the job," I advise her. I emphasize "decline": I'm communicating, to Lorna, smoking madly, and to Mike, who looks like he wants to suck his thumb, that I, at least, am behaving like an adult.

In reaction, Carrie's eyes bulge. Mouth open, too, she looks like the girl on a horror movie poster. If Dad could see her now, his illusions of Carrie-the-Competent would finally fall away. He'd see Carrie for who she really is—a passive-aggressive freak who always has to be in charge.

When Mom was sick, Carrie drew up a visiting schedule, turning our own house into a hospital. She had one of those fat pens where you can change the color cartridge by clicking, and she assigned different colors to Lorna, me, and her. When I complained to Mom about Carrie dictating what time we spent with her, she said, "Oh hon. It makes her feel better, having something to do." Then she tousled my hair and said, "How about not arguing with your sister?"

Arguing: we heard that verb a lot as a kid, often hissed by our father. "Don't argue! Your mother is trying to sleep!" To this day, Dad acts like arguing is calamitous, something only savages do. When I asked, composedly, why he'd chosen Carrie to be the executor, he looked aghast, as if I'd poured gasoline on his chair and torched it.

———

Six months ago, Dad's and Gillian's Christmas card had contained a check for $15,000. The typed letter wrapped around the check had read rather cryptically, "If this card contains a check, the money is our attempt to even things out, to treat our children fairly. If this card does not contain a check, consider our loans to you forgiven."

I wagered that we were the only ones to receive a check, but Grant thought Lorna might have received a smaller check, say a couple grand at least. "What could she have spent $15,000 on?" he said. "Doesn't she buy everything she owns from secondhand stores?"

"Booze. Marty. A DUI," I said. The DUI is a conjecture, but it's not wild guesswork. Lorna's only been in AA for about eight months now, since November, and Dad was clearly worried about her at Thanksgiving. Lorna bounces between problems the way Shane's ex-wife Sherilynn did fashion trends. When Lorna was a kid, the rest of us shared a secret candy stash behind the waffle maker in a high cabinet Lorna couldn't reach. This was for her own good, Dad said, because Lorna had "self-control issues," and it was mean to eat candy in front of her. Then in high school, she became bulimic and so thin that one time she was wearing these drawstring pants and they came untied and literally fell to her ankles when she stood from the table at breakfast. After high school, she stopped vomiting and gained the weight back, but she moved in with a jackass named Marty who played video games in his boxers while she worked at a yarn store. Then there was that time she called Dad from Mexico because she lost her ID and couldn't get back across the border.

Neither of us doubted that Shane and Mike had "borrowed" $15,000 plus from Dad and Gillian over the years.

And now Shane has the gall to suggest that I should decline being executor of Dad's and Gillian's will? As if there's anyone else in this family who is responsible enough to take my place.

Feeling a little feisty from the mojitos, I say, "And what? Nominate you, Shane? Or how about Lorna? You think she'd make a good executor?"

———

The thing about the number three: someone is always being left out. Oh, there are isolated moments that can be harmonious—say, the three of us would briefly have a good time playing Monopoly—but twenty-five minutes in, Lorna would be crying about landing on Waterworks and rolling a twelve, and Carrie would be commenting on the irony of crying about Waterworks, and Lorna and I would be united, again, over what a pretentious, pleased-with-herself shithead Carrie was. Or every so often, Carrie and Lorna, though normally as compatible as a cactus and a kitten, would be bonding in some girl way—baking Tollhouse cookies, knitting these ridiculous beanie hats—and I would be the little match girl stuck outside in the snow, peering in.

It's not just siblings, either. Every time I get together with my friends Todd and Ollie, sooner or later, the evening ends with one sticking his lip out. Something about the number three: it's like a law of nature.

You'd think that when Dad married Gillian and Mike got introduced into the mix that would have resolved our triangulation dynamic. But Mike is too much of a potato to count as a full-fledged entity. His entry into our lives was less like converting a three-legged stool into a stable, four-legged chair than like sticking a wad of rolled-up newspaper under one of the stool legs to make it that much more tippy.

Though I have to say, it's not so much that Lorna and I choose each other than Carrie shoves us forcibly together. Like when we used to play badminton and Carrie would always want to be solo. "You and Lorna be partners!" she'd trill. That's how I feel when Lorna straightens up from her hunched vulture posture and says, "And why wouldn't I be a good executor? For fuck's sake, Carrie!"

Her wedge of a face has gone red, like it always does when she gets mad. We used to call her Heat Miser. But "for fuck's sake" cracks the three of us up. Not Mike, of course, who sits there looking back and forth between Lorna and Carrie and me with his mouth half open. If there were subtitles to Mike's thoughts, those subtitles would all say "Doh?"

"Fuck!" I say. "Poor Fuck." Fuck was what Shane and I used to call Lorna's hamster Chuck. Because after her first stroke, Mom struggled with pronouncing various sounds. She developed this weird way of pronouncing "ch" so that the sound was more like "f." So when Mom would get on Lorna about the hamster "Lorna, did you change out Chuck's wood chips?" what we heard was "Lorna, did you fange out Fuck's wood fips?" When Mom wasn't around, Shane and I would say to Lorna, "For Fuck's sake, fange out the wood fips, Lorna!"

Then one time Mom overheard us. Her face turned red as fast as flipping the switch to turn on Christmas lights. That's where Lorna gets it from. She has super pale skin like Mom did. Any bit of blood rushing to the surface stands out like blood on snow. When Mom overheard us, she turned red, but she didn't say a word for a long moment. Then she said, quietly and without emotion, "I'm going to be too busy with medical treatments to stay on top of making sure this hamster stays alive. You're going to have to remember to take care of him, Lorna. Or you two are going to have to help her. Either that or he's going to end up dead."

One might think that moment would have been the kick in the teeth Lorna needed, or Shane and me, for that matter. But Lorna was five at the time, I was ten, Shane eleven. Even if it weren't for the distraction of all of Mom's medical issues, we probably wouldn't have been responsible enough to keep a hamster alive on our own.

A Paul Simon song blares out of the speakers, startling every one of us. Robert comes running over to me, his palms pressed so hard against his ears that he looks like he's trying to squeeze something out of his skull, like his head is a giant pimple he's trying to pop.

The volume is quickly reduced, and Grant steps out and apologizes. He's followed by Gillian, who is carrying a tray with guacamole and chips and grapes. The guacamole, we all know, will contain sour cream. Because that's how Mike likes it, Shane has said. But maybe it's just because that's how Gillian's always made it. Maybe Mike liking it that way is secondary.

—

"Where's Dad?" asks Lorna, and Gillian makes the strangest face—it's as if someone goosed her behind. That's an expression of Mom's that always killed me. I could never figure out what a goose had to do with pinching. Geese don't have fingers.

"Doug's resting. He'll be out in a second," Gillian says. "Who needs another drink?" She takes everyone's orders and heads back to the house.

Carrie's husband takes a seat in that strange, swamp creature way Grant has, like sitting is a ten-step process. He's three years older than me, but he acts like he's seventy. Do not get that man talking about composting. Seriously, your ears will slide off your head.

"You all should be less focused on the fact that I got assigned the thankless task of being executor, and more on what the job actually is," says Carrie, speaking double-time. "If you were listening to Dad actually describe the will, you'd know this is basic. Gillian inherits everything when he dies, and then when she dies, it all goes to the four of us, in equal quarters. All I am is the knife slicing the cake into four equal pieces." She makes a slicing gesture.

"Well, that's a revealing metaphor, that you're a knife," I point out. I reflect on how coolly Carrie just referred to Dad's and Gillian's deaths.

"A knife slicing cake, not a knife stabbing you," says Carrie, rolling her eyes.

"What about that percent of the estate executors get?" I ask, because I actually know a thing or two. Grant looks like he wishes Dad and Gillian would assign him some other complicated task—rewiring their electricity, shingling their roof—so he could vanish.

"I'll gift that one percent back to the estate. That will be part of the cake."

So I'm momentarily at a loss for words, but then Lorna shakes her head. "Guys. You're like the White House reporters, getting distracted because of some stupid Trump tweet and forgetting the real issue." Lorna was always a basket case, one problem after another as a kid; she could hardly put on her own socks. But when she applied herself—Mom's word, again, as if Lorna were some kind of robot—she could be clever. "Why is Dad so sure he's dying first? Did you hear him say, 'When I pass away,' like that's a given? Why haul us all here in the middle of June to talk about his will? He's sixty-three. Whence the urgency?" She pauses. "Why the fuck is he 'resting'?"

Carrie and Lorna and I look at each other. I remember that year and a half after Mom died, before Dad started dating Gillian. To call us latchkey kids puts it way too mildly. We were feral. Dad would come home late, leaving it up to us to do our homework, take care of poor doomed hamster #2 (the first, Fuck Chuck, died of starvation most likely, a couple of months before Mom died) and feed ourselves dinner. The shit we had for dinner! Carrie would try to establish some semblance of order—iceberg lettuce with Paul Newman's ranch dressing, or she'd fry up Steak-umms or boil ramen—but half the time, dinner was popcorn and Moon Pies. I will never forget the chaos of trying to get Lorna to brush her teeth, Carrie holding her down while I squeezed toothpaste and Lorna turned a shade of tomato.

"Spy club," Lorna says, and sticks out one freckled arm. Our code from the bad old days, trying to figure out first what the hell was going on with Mom, why she was talking like her mouth was full of mashed potatoes. You hear about kids being raised by wolves, but the three of us were raised by kitchen cabinets and vacuum cleaners—nothing sentient. Carrie sighs, and sticks out her right arm too, and I do as well. Even Mike does, though with that guy, he's probably just stretching.

———

Of course, it's entirely normal that Dad's tired still from the hip surgery two months ago. The man fell off a ladder pruning a tree, gave himself and Gillian a serious scare. I mean, surgery to replace his bone! There's the limited mobility as he recovers. The pain. And no doubt he's a little depressed too. He hasn't missed a run more than two days straight in all his adult life. For Dad, six weeks without running is kind of like six weeks without seeing the sun in the sky or six weeks without laughter or six weeks without the taste of something sweet. And while he's gone on a couple of short runs this past week, they were anything but pleasant, he told me.

For years Gillian has been on him about not pruning that tree himself. She even called me once and asked me to talk sense into him about calling a landscaper. But Dad, always stubborn, kept right on pruning the tree.

Shane and Lorna have never seemed particularly attuned to Dad as a whole person, though, as someone more than simply their father. Strange given how absent he was after Mom died.

Sometimes I wonder too if they think the man is immortal. Again strange, considering Mom was only thirty-seven when she died. And don't they recognize that men collectively die younger than women? That Dad outlived Mom is already atypical. What are the fucking odds he's going to outlive Gillian too, when in addition to women in this country having a life expectancy five years greater than that of men, she's also three years younger than him?

Not that I plan to say any of this to Shane and Lorna. Finally, they're focused on something other than my being executor of the will. Let them spy on Dad. Maybe they'll bring Lenny into their spy club so that he'll finally have something better to do than imprison lightning bugs in his overcrowded penitentiary. Then while Lenny's peeking through bedroom windows or pressing his ear against Dad's door, Robert and I can free the unjustly incarcerated.

—

It bums me out to think about Dad being really sick, but of course it makes all kinds of sense—really, it's the only possible conclusion. That's the reason for that fucked up "Consider our loans forgiven" card at Christmas; that's the reason we are summoned to Fairfield, like Dad's some old time English king. When Mom was sick—well, once she really accepted dying, and wasn't so cranky and aggrieved about it—weirdly enough, those were some of my nicest memories of her. I'd lie in her bed, and while she napped, I'd blow up Space Invaders or thumb through a stack of comic books. Sometimes when she'd wake up, I'd read them to her. "That guy looks like a thug," she'd say. Like, no shit, Mom, that's Two Face, he's an arch villain. She cracked me up.

I picture Dad, lying in bed, and, for once, peaceful and softened. I picture straightening the covers and folding them neatly over his chest. I could make him toast and cut off the crusts. We could play chess together. He would be still, for once—actually present.

I catch Carrie looking at me. "We'll figure it out," I reassure her.

She says, "Hey, go for it." Bossy and difficult as Carrie can be, she's scared for Dad, I can tell, and grateful that I'm on top of this. In the end, Carrie wants to be looked after. That's why she married boring Grant, instead of that dude Ted with the Harley and the tattoo of a jellyfish on his bicep. Carrie wants someone dependable. Which makes sense, given all the craziness we grew up with, having to practically raise ourselves. Our sheets would smell so bad because no one ever washed them. I remember lying in bed, wondering what smelled so funky. Every so often I'll walk by a homeless person and that smell wafts back to me.

Carrie is OCD, according to my ex-wife Sherilynn—Sherilynn is always diagnosing people, like being a Psych minor in college gives her insight. Carrie's son Robert, Sherilynn maintained, was on the spectrum. Who knows with that weird kid?

Constantly deflecting my son's efforts to play with him, to get him interested in nature. Lenny keeps trying, though; he's a good kid, inclusive.

So, I smile back at Carrie, to let her know I've got this. That she can lay down her burdens, like it says in the hymn, because her older brother's here.

———

Gillian comes out with a tray full of refreshed mojitos, and limeades for Lorna and the kids. As she hands Mike his mojito, he says, "Mom, any speculation as to just how much we stand to inherit?"

Shane gives Mike a look like he just suggested we murder Dad in his sleep, then search his pockets. But I know Shane's curious, too. I can almost feel his ears stretch, like a vine creeping up a tree trunk to reach more sunlight.

Gillian says matter-of-factly, "We've agreed to not discuss figures. One, you can't account for the unexpected, as you all know. I don't want to tell you one thing and then have to disappoint you if our situation changes. Two, we think you're better off not counting on some future inheritance. We think it's for your own good." She picks up the empty glasses scattered on the table. Then she says, "I'm going to go get the brie and crackers." She smiles.

Shane says, "Hold up. By unexpected, you mean like medical expenses?"

"Well, sure. Or if the cost of living greatly increases. Or our government seizes everyone's bank accounts." Gillian laughs.

One time we were all making fun of the dumb family decals on other people's automobiles. Then Lorna got serious, said, "What happens when someone dies? Do they scratch her off the car?" I remember her pinching the skin on her neck so hard she left fingernail indentations, like tally marks all over her neck. Tally marks that I imagined represented all the things she worried about. Gillian's reply: "Or what if advertising the contents of their families like that only helps ensure that when they're targeted by a psycho killer, he can be sure to pick off every one of them? Not overlook the one hiding under the bed or in the closet?" Then Gillian cackled.

Now Lorna is picking at her neck again. "Seize our accounts?!"

What I think: Does Lorna have any money for the government to steal? Talk about getting distracted from the real issue.

Shane says, "What's going on with Dad? If he's sick, that's something that is most definitely not in our best interest to withhold. We deserve to know. We have a right to know."

Everyone's eyes are on Gillian. Even Lenny has stopped swinging his arms in the air like King Kong. He's still and quiet for the first time all day, the first time in his life maybe.

About a year after Mom died, Dad started, for the first time, going to church. I thought it was about trying to find solace, to be in a place where he could more easily imagine meeting Mom again someday—a place at any rate where he'd have company in that kind of fantasy. Once, Lorna asked me where Mom was, and Dad overheard me say, "Rotting in the ground." He got all kinds of bent out of shape.

But Carrie's theory—and I have to give her credit for coming up with it pretty much immediately—was that he started going to church to find a new wife. "You've watched *The Sound of Music* too many times," I told her, and she scoffed and pointed out a church was not a convent, and no reasonable person went to a convent to find a wife. "Anyway, it's better than going to a bar," she said. Eleven-year-old Carrie, already world-wise. And sure enough, two months later, Dad was dating Gillian.

On the whole, we were thumbs up on Gillian. She was funny. She made cool desserts, like rainbow Jell-O—that was a twenty-four-hour procedure, where she'd use a glass bowl and make one color layer at a time, pour in the lemon when the lime had hardened and so forth. She even put in canned fruit that was the same color palette—mandarin oranges in the orange layer, sour cherries in the red layer. Carrie called it white trash food, but Lorna and I were appreciative, after having spent a year scavenging, eating s'mores for dinner, but terrible s'mores, saltine crackers instead of graham crackers because that's all we had.

But Gillian did have what we all called the Death Stare, and she aims that at me now.

"What an odd comment to make, Shane," Gillian says. She sets the tray of empty glasses down on the table.

I stare back at her. "What a non-answer, Gillian," I say.

And there's an electric-static silence, before Grant coughs and says, like a grandpa, "Now, now." I have never understood that reprimand. What's it supposed to mean? To call one back into the present, reorient one to now, like pushing a "refresh" button? I suspect the expression is code for let go of the past, but that's another concept I've never understood. The past is what composes us. That's like telling a house to let go of its nails and wood.

———

I write a mental sticky note to remind Grant to please never ever say "now, now" again, that I can only take so much of that terrible phrase before I reach my limit and detonate like one of the little Christmas ornament-looking explosives in Candy Crush.

Then there's the sound of the sliding glass door, and there's Dad. He's got a cake in his hands. He's grinning.

Gillian says, "But we haven't had dinner yet."

Dad says, "So? Anyone else object?"

Grant objects to cake on pretty much all occasions—people and their processed sugar, he says; why not choose fruit if you want something sweet?—but he doesn't say anything. Neither does anyone else. Dad's recently become a fantastic baker. When I say fantastic, I mean like *Baking Show* fantastic. When I said something about picking up a cake for Robert's sixth birthday, Dad was all I've-got-this. He had a "consultation" with Robert, and then the day of the party he showed up with a cake replica of the Titanic, complete with an iceberg, both of which sat on this glittery blue glaze that included fondant rafts and people. The people all looked terrified which, to be fair, is probably accurate, but it also made me wonder if Gillian had a hand in their crafting.

Robert's friends went nuts over those fondant people, though. They played with them like they were action figures. Enacted scenes, which basically boiled down to screams of mass hysteria. "Women and children first! Women and children first!" Robert yelled.

Shane was icy in his comment on the photos on Facebook, clearly stung that Dad hadn't offered to make Lenny's cake a couple months earlier. My pointing out that I lived forty minutes away from Dad versus his six-hour commute didn't do much to ease his mind.

The other thing that pissed off Shane was that when we were kids, the only thing Dad cooked was hamburgers. And then after Mom died, not even hamburgers. "What the fuck was up with that?" Shane messaged me. "We could have starved to death! And now he's making a cake Titanic?!"

This cake is no ordinary weekend's baking either. It's a stack of freaking crêpes. I count sixteen. Layered between the crêpes is some kind of cream like you'd find in an éclair. The whole thing is covered in chocolate and decorated with raspberries.

As we're chewing, I feel Shane's and Lorna's thoughts ticking. Cake before dinner? Crêpes? What does this mean?!

Then when I compliment the cake, Dad says, "I made it early this morning before you guys got here."

Gillian shakes her head. "He was up at 5 a.m. making crêpes! I couldn't sleep with all the clatter in the kitchen, and then he slapped my hand when I went to grab one!"

"Wow, this is really good, Gramps," says my nephew Robert. I shoot Lenny, gobbling up this bizarre IHOP cake, a look: he is not to be outdone by his weirdo spectrum cousin. Lenny swallows—he has so much cake in his mouth that the effect is of an ostrich swallowing a watermelon—coughs, and says, "Yes, excellent cake, Gramps. Thank you so much." I grin at Carrie, to communicate that my kid has better manners. Even if he does have chocolate all around his mouth like Bozo the Clown.

Carrie surprises me by smiling back. Our smiles are a rope ladder between us, something I can climb and finally reach my sister—she has some unflattering salad bowl haircut that makes her look like a toadstool. Cake before dinner? My eyes communicate to her. Her smile widens, but it's an inviting smile, not a malicious one. So what if we have cake before dinner? Her eyes flash back. Dinner will be something weird with sour cream. Enjoy!

I look at Dad, daintily forking a raspberry into his mouth. His cheeks are pink, flushed with pleasure. He's proud of his cake.

When we were kids, Dad used to want us to open our big Christmas present Christmas Eve. "Wait until tomorrow, Doug," Mom would say, and he'd say, "The kids want to open one now, though!" But he was the one; he wanted us to open it right now.

Cake before dinner: it occurs to me that my life is like a film where they get the reels mixed up, and everything happens out of order. When I was a kid, I had no real parents to speak of—one dying, the other absent. I scrounged for everything, including affection. I was like a filthy, gobbling pigeon. And now I have a pink-cheeked father who bakes cake. I was a father before I was a husband—Sherilynn and I only married when Lenny was almost two—and by the time he was six, she had taken off. We got along better when I was traveling all the time for work and we saw much less of each other. "Familiarity breeds disgust": the parting words of my ex-wife. But Lenny is doing much better without a mother than I did—well, a mother in California, versus permanently distant. He has a father who cooks and reads him books. He drew his family for second grade, and I have to say, it pleased me to see that "family" consisted of me and Lenny, holding hands—these fucked up hands that looked like rakes. Partly because Sherilynn didn't deserve to be in the picture, but also partly because it made me feel like Yeah, we're doing okay.

Now, if I were drawing a family, it would have to include this whole clown car. I look all around the table, taking them in. My dad, with his very pink cheeks; Gillian, patting a napkin to her mouth; caved-in Mike, the posture of a koala bear; messy Lorna, the human tumbleweed; Carrie with her funky toadstool haircut; Grant, with his round glasses—I'd make those glasses look like bubbles; Robert, for the first time today cheerful—I'd draw a big blue smile on that strange kid; my son, with his plastic bin of lightning bugs. I'd draw each bug—curls for wings, a yellow dot for every mystifying chemical reaction.

ACCOUNTABILITY BUDDIES

WHEN DONNA BRINGS HOME THE EXERCISE book from the library, her eight-year-old daughter Tess says of the bare-stomached woman on the book's cover, "Sexy! She's got six-pack abs!"

Donna looks at the abs in question. What she sees is caterpillar poop. Donna's backyard vegetable garden is sprinkled with ridged caterpillar turds, like tiny grenades. That's because the tree branches that reach out over the garden are infested with giant green caterpillars bigger than her husband Theo's thick fingers.

"What do you mean, 'Sexy'?" Donna strokes her daughter's hair, which is tangled as usual. "Where'd you hear that word?"

For that matter, where did Tess hear "abs" and "six-pack"? Are these terms eight-year-olds lightly toss around? She wants to ask her friend Lynette—Lynette has a daughter six months older than Tess, and often the two women will exchange the words their children say. Except, come to think of it, Lynette will be judge-y. There's a pattern to the words Lynette's kid says, and the subtext is that they're all signs of Giselle's incipient genius. Only a brilliant not-quite-nine-year-old would know about convection ovens; only a prodigy would describe herself, when she fell off her bike, as being "wounded." Whereas a kid who says "sexy" and "abs" sounds like a kid who's watched too many Kardashians slither and flex, a kid who will grow into a tween who wears tiny shorts that barely cover her ass.

Donna loves Lynette, but Lynette is challenging. "Love" may in fact be the wrong word. Donna "has" Lynette, like her yard has trees that are stressful to sit under because of the risk of being defecated upon by caterpillars.

Lynette is in fact why Donna checked this exercise book out from the library. Lynette asked Donna to be her accountability buddy. The deal is Lynette's going to vlog about DIY crafts projects three days a week, and Donna's job is to nudge her toward success by touching base and encouraging her. But to make this whole accountability buddy thing work, Lynette said it has to be balanced. "You have to have a goal of your own that I help you with. Otherwise, probably I'll just get annoyed with you pestering me about the vlog," Lynette said. A warning bell instantly went off in Donna's head, like it did every time she got tempted to vent to Lynette about some grievance she had with Theo. Venting about Theo's selfishness in bed or the time he spends on social media feels satisfying in the moment, but Lynette pockets every insult, every fault. Then, weeks later,

Lynette will say of her Ray, "Sex has been incredible lately!" or "Did I tell you Ray has this new thing where he doesn't touch his phone or the computer all weekend? Instead, he made sourdough bread from scratch!"

This accountability buddy thing is going to come back to bite her, too.

Donna tries to remember if getting in shape was even her idea; she suspects not. Donna worries sometimes about her brain—a tumor or early onset Alzheimer's—but she is nearly positive she proposed completing that knitting project she began over a year ago and promptly gave up. Because what on earth is more monotonous than knitting a sweater? Well, exercise for one. And didn't Lynette then purse her lips and say, "Hmm. You could do that. Or! What about getting into shape?" Maybe Lynette didn't even say it, but thought it, and beamed that thought at Donna, via her pursed lips and a certain you-can-do-better cast to her face. Donna grew up with a highly manipulative mother who was always chasing cults—her mother had both wanted to control Donna and her various husbands but had longed to be told what to do herself—and that made Donna particularly susceptible to subtle forms of mind control.

"What's wrong with 'sexy'?" Tess says now, confused. "It's not a bad word."

"Not bad, exactly. But, well, remember back when we saw *Sleeping Beauty*, and the first fairy gives baby Aurora the gift of beauty, and the second one gives her the gift of song? And I said, man, that gift sucks, I can think of about eight hundred gifts I would rather have than the gift of song?"

"'*Sucks*' is a bad word," Tess says, coldly. "Giselle started a sexy club. Only sexy girls can join. Right now, it's me, Giselle, Annie Pruitt, and Carmen. I'm sexy because of my lips."

What Donna was about to say was that she'd been wrong to single out the suckiness of the gift of song. She wanted to say something about how tricky beauty is, how easily it fools us into giving up our values, our dignity. She was going to tell Tess about the Greek goddess Hera, how she turned away her son, Hephaestus, because he had a deformed foot—in other words, because she deemed him ugly.

But now Donna is preoccupied with her daughter's self-claimed sexy lips. Granted, Tess does have nice lips. She's inherited Donna's lips, and the truth is Donna has long recognized them as one of her best features. Did she think this at the age of eight? Donna doesn't think so, but her memory, of course, is shit. She does recall thinking as a girl how grateful she was that she didn't inherit her own mother's lips, which were so thin they made her think of the drawn-on black line of her Raggedy Ann doll's lips. Kissing a mouth like that would be like kissing the rigid trashcan mouth of Pac-Man. Almost no cushion over the teeth.

"Who decided your lips are sexy? Giselle?" Donna suppresses a smile. Oh, how she will enjoy telling Lynette about how her little prodigy is herding her fellow third graders into Sexy Club. It's the first time in months that Donna has looked forward to calling Lynette. She imagines her own voice (concerned but severe) delivering news that will land like one of those grenade-shaped caterpillar turds.

WAR

 at the base, and I can't decide if he's interesting or creepy. The day he knocks on our door to introduce himself, he teaches me War—not the boring card game my little sister Greta likes, but Charley's design. Creatures are our soldiers. Using his mother's pasta strainer, we wade in the stream and catch a heap of tadpoles. Charley dumps them on the grass, then lifts a rock high over his head. The rock is thick and streaky like a steak. I jump backwards when Charley drops it.

"Hiroshima," he says. He picks up the rock to count casualties. The tadpoles are flattened discs. They look like sticky M&Ms.

Only one tadpole survives. The tip of its tail is mangled like a utensil Dad doesn't see before he turns on the garbage disposal. But the animal is otherwise intact.

"Radiation exposure," Charley says. "Even if he makes it through the next few days, he'll die later of cancer." He smashes the tadpole beneath his sneaker. "It's the humane thing to do," he adds.

I know not to tell Mom about War when she asks me if I had fun playing with Charley. I say, "Sure," and I go to my room, which is stacked with boxes I haven't unpacked.

In one box is a framed photo of me and Ruth in matching Wonder Woman costumes. I haven't seen her in nearly a year, not since her dad died in Afghanistan and she and her mother moved off base to live with Ruth's grandparents in Detroit.

When I told Ruth that my cousin Anna didn't find out about death until she was nearly ten, Ruth was stunned. "How is it possible to live in this world and not know about death?" That was before her dad died. I shrugged and said that my cousin's parents weren't military. Anna lives in a rich suburb of Chicago. Her parents were determined for her childhood to be "untarnished." Or that's how Mom put it when she complained to Dad about my cousin explaining that her dead hamster was merely sleeping.

"Holly is in denial," Mom said, of her sister. "Did I tell you she refused to read Anna *Charlotte's Web*? I asked her why, and she said, 'I'm not reading my kid a book where the first sentence has someone holding an ax!'"

"That's the one about the pig?" Dad asked.

Mom ruffled his hair and said, "The man has actually read a book!"

Mom's different now, since we relocated to North Carolina—more specifically, since Dad was redeployed. Ours is the only house on the street without a flag. When I asked her why, she shook her head and muttered something about true believers.

I suspect what she feels regarding Aunt Holly these days is closer to envy.

The Hiroshima rock produces the most casualties in a single blow, but I bet Mom would be more upset watching us play Vietnam. We use a magnifying glass to set ants on fire. "Napalm," Charley calls it.

The Morton Salt we shake on three banana slugs is poison gas. It's 1917, and the slugs cower in the trenches, too shell-shocked and disoriented to fasten their masks.

I watched Mom kill plenty of ants and slugs when they got into her vegetable garden back in Texas. She seemed to take pleasure in it, too. When I asked her how diatomaceous earth worked, she said, without batting an eye, "It absorbs the protective coating on their exoskeletons. Basically, their insides dry and shrivel like raisins."

But that was before Ruth's dad. That week, after the news came, Mom's vegetable garden dried up like the insides of the ants she'd poisoned. She didn't even bother to harvest the last of the tomatoes. They browned and wrinkled on the plants' withered stems. They looked like the bindles cartoon hobos prop onto their shoulders when they leave town.

Sometimes I feel ashamed playing War with Charley. I wonder if he's a budding psychopath, and if that makes me one, too. Like when Charley and I conscript two crickets into Civil War soldiers, brothers bent on destroying each other. Charley's cricket is Constantine the Yankee, mine is Ambrose the Confederate. Charley spears Ambrose with a toothpick, then snaps off one of his delicate, hinged legs. "Amputated without anesthesia, because the hospital has used up its chloroform supply," Charley says. "Not that it will save him: the gangrene has already set in, he'll be dead within a week."

Or worse: the day we turn a fat grub into a suicide bomber by rubber-banding it to a firecracker. I'm the one who lights the fuse and drops the grub onto a pile of earthworms. Because suicide bomber is my idea. Because that's how Ruth's dad was blown up.

Other times I think War is just Charley and me hardening off, the way Mom used to gradually expose seedlings she grew indoors to the "elements"—harsh sun, dry air, cold nights. The plants had to be introduced gradually, she said, so they'd become hardy. So they'd survive.

AIRSHIP

 notes on the spare side, limited in their delivery of information. "Taking off. Pls look after Zazu," a Post-it gummed to the toaster, did not fill him with any particular alarm. He made himself coffee, and when Zazu padded into the kitchen in her footsie pajamas, helped her pour milk into her bowl of sugar pops, sniffing the carton first because it was a couple of days past its expiration date. It smelled okay. Zazu, like many children of users, was good at being quiet. The only noise that emitted from her end of the table was the soft clink of her plastic spoon. It wasn't until Drew looked at his watch and realized he needed to be at the hotel in twenty minutes for his shift that he picked up Renata's note again and processed that "taking off" had no endpoint, nor did "Pls look after Zazu."

Renata had freaked out last fall when the form for preschool required no fewer than three emergency contacts. "As if this country isn't hard enough on mothers already, now I have to feel deficient *because* I don't have any help?" When she'd put

Drew down as emergency contact #1, he'd sheepishly asked if that meant Renata expected him to take custody of Zazu if something happened to Renata. (For emergency contact #2, Renata had written in the name of the city's mayor and his phone number at City Hall. For #3 she had written in the chief of police.) This had been before they'd moved in together, before they'd had boring sex, the kind of sex he would have sworn back then wasn't possible with Renata. Like how it wasn't possible for something with sugar as its primary ingredient to taste anything other than sweet. Renata had said, "No, asshole." Then, "But you would, wouldn't you?"

Drew couldn't very well rely on the mayor or the chief of police for last-minute babysitting, so he told Zazu to get dressed and pack some toys: he was going to have to stash her behind the hotel's reception desk and hope Susan, the manager, either didn't find out or that she was fonder of kids than she was adults.

It took Zazu less than two minutes to load into her backpack her elephant, a box of crayons, and a *Dora the Explorer* coloring book Renata had got her at Goodwill that depressed Drew because it had already been partly filled in. That had been his most recent dispute with Renata. "Who cares? She'll color it in herself soon enough," Renata had said. Which escalated into a diatribe against pointless consumerism and the military-industrial complex, and who the hell did Drew think he was, questioning her parenting choices? To Drew, giving a child a coloring book where the monkey's boots were already filled in, and messily, by an artist who did not draw inside the lines, and on top of that, used the wrong color—brown, not red—well, it was like giving someone a stem with the flower yanked off.

But he'd backed off once he realized how angry Renata was.

Anyway, Drew recognized it didn't make much sense to be shocked by the coloring book. He'd packed bowls for Renata when Zazu had been five feet away, clicking together her Duplos. Or there was that time when they'd been screwing, Renata on top of him, and he saw Zazu standing in the open bedroom door. Renata, without twisting her torso, had said, "You know where the water glasses are." She'd then gotten gruff with Drew too. His dick had gone soft at the sight of Zazu, her pajamas streaked with toothpaste stains.

Only when Drew opened the car door and confronted the empty to-go cups, wadded fast-food napkins, and a collection of animal bones—steer mostly, but also deer—he'd gotten from his friend Mal for a garden project he was planning as a surprise for his mother's birthday, did he remember that he didn't have a child's car seat. That Renata hadn't transferred Zazu's seat could be a promising sign, but it could also mean that Renata simply wasn't thinking about Zazu at all. Either way, no car seat meant Zazu was going to have to ride all the way to the hotel without even a seatbelt holding her in because a seatbelt, he knew, could strangle her or, worse, slice off her head.

"I'll drive carefully," he said. "But maybe ride with your arms out in front of you to brace yourself against my seat in case I have to hit the brakes? Better your arms than your head."

Zazu didn't ask what he meant by this. Like a person used to making do with strange and inadequate methods of self-preservation, she dutifully held her arms out, palms facing his seat.

Drew thought of the reflective, neon orange runner's vest his mother wore if she had to be out of the house after dark. How at odds that vest was with his mother, a timid woman who shriveled when attention veered her way. But visibility was a price she was willing to pay to stay safe. He remembered her one friend, a knobby woman named Deirdre, telling his mother over flowery smelling tea that bright colors conveyed confidence and that confidence deterred predators. He'd been flipping through Deirdre's *National Geographics*, admiring images of Portuguese man-of-war. Their poisonous tentacles glowed iridescent blue in the dark.

In the house, he didn't mind Zazu's stoicism. He appreciated how un-childlike she was in that regard. But in the cramped space of the car, the animal bones rattling on the seat beside her, Zazu's silence was unnerving.

"What do you think that sculpture is supposed to be? A zebra or a horse?" he said as they drove past a park. The animal was all skeleton, its steel bones painted a matte red. Three massive ravens perched along its spine, one crooking its wings. With the birds squatting on it, the sculpture reminded Drew of another

National Geographic image: the picked ribcage of a wildebeest like a table decoration around which a group of vultures gathered.

"Mama says mule," Zazu said. Then, as if invoking Renata had made Zazu for the first time consider her, "Where is Mama?"

Drew glanced at her face in the rearview mirror, then looked away. Zazu didn't appear to be verging on tears, nor was the question purely casual. What to say?

When he'd phoned Renata, while Zazu assembled her backpack, his call had gone straight to voicemail. He had yet to hear a ping from his phone indicating any response to his barrage of texts, all iterations on Zazu's question ("Where R U?" "Where the fuck R U?" "?!?"). Getting loaded was the obvious conclusion. Or maybe that part was past tense, and now she'd simply lost track of time.

Ever since he'd first seen Renata, at Coco Loco's last June, wearing a cropped metallic top exposing a cummerbund of gleaming belly, she'd messed with Drew's experience of time. He would descend from a high, his head on her lap, and be amazed to find it was late afternoon. Time spent with Renata was taffy: stretchy and sticky.

"I don't know, Zaz," he said, finally, and pulled into the parking lot of The Oasis.

"Is this where we're staying now?" Zazu said, staring out at the pink building—coral, his manager, Susan, called the color. Two palm trees flanked the entrance, but you had to squint to

spot another living thing on the street that wasn't human or pigeon or roadkill—the latter, of course, not technically alive.

"Staying?" Drew said.

Zazu nodded.

"What? No, no. This is the hotel where I work," Drew said.
"And you can drop your arms now," he added. "Nobody's going to
hit us while we're parked here."

Of course, someone could. Car accidents supposedly happened most frequently within a mile from a person's house or
place of employment. The reason: you get comfortable and let
your guard down.

Now that he was in the parking lot of The Oasis, Drew was
less confident about his plan to stash Zazu behind the desk. The
odds of Susan neither finding out nor minding weren't much
better than the odds that Renata would turn up sober, with a le-
gitimate excuse for why she left Zazu with him, despite knowing
damn well he had to work.

"Zaz, I need you to stay out in the car, just for a bit. I'll roll
the windows down. I'll bring you some water and snacks. And
I'll be able to see you through the window the whole time, so if
you need to use the bathroom or if you need anything at all, just
wave, okay?"

His friend Mal's sole job duty at the casino was to patrol the
parking lot, writing down the license plates of vehicles in which
children had been left. Drew's jaw had gone slack when Mal told

him this. That was before Drew met Renata.

"I need to use the bathroom now," Zazu said.

Drew sighed. "Bathroom" was operating like "Mama" had a few minutes ago: saying the word invoked the recognition of a need. It was like the opening of Genesis, God enunciating the world into being: Let there be light.

"Okay," he said. "You remember the peanut floor place? You remember that game you play, how to be invisible? That game you play really, really well?" The peanut floor place was the dive bar down the street from Renata's house. He and Renata often went there after Zazu fell asleep, Renata reasoning that leaving Zazu in the house by herself for an hour or so was fine; the bar was only two blocks away; the distance was no different, really, than if they lived in an extremely large mansion. But several times Zazu had come with them, and it was true, the kid had a special talent for blending into backgrounds. She played on the floor with the husks of peanut shells so unobtrusively that not only did the bartender not notice her and chuck them all out, Drew forgot about her himself. The kid's spirit animal, Drew reflected, was a chameleon.

Zazu nodded.

"This hotel is like that, okay? Go invisible. We walk in, you head straight to the back of the lobby. You'll see the bathroom next to the elevators. Make sure you go to the one with the picture of the lady on the door."

When he'd been a kid, his mother hadn't let him go into

a men's restroom until he was so old that women were giving the two of them dirty looks. His mother had been wary of men, even men she knew, like Ted Tester, Drew's friend Wyatt's dad. The man would drive Drew home after a sleepover, walk him to the door, and Drew's mother would barely open the door wide enough to let Drew into the apartment or long enough to say thank you to Mr. Tester before she shut it again. Then she'd launch into questions about whether anything weird had happened at Wyatt's house: Did anyone touch him? Did anyone say something to him that made him uncomfortable? By "anyone," he'd understood that she meant Mr. Tester.

As for bathrooms, she didn't say what precisely might happen to him in there, but when she did finally give in and send him to the men's, she demanded first that he look her in the eye, and then she told him to be careful and to always be aware of his surroundings. *It's like she thinks she's shipping you off to Iraq*, Wyatt had said.

Now as Zazu got out of the car, she said, "Mama hates that word."

"Don't I know it," Drew said. Renata had once given him a lecture about how in Old English, "lady" literally meant "bread maker." *Do I look like a fucking bread maker to you?*

He told Zaz to discreetly return to the car when she was done. He'd meet her out there with the water and snacks.

Jamie had had the night shift and, as usual, she was zonked.

As Drew grabbed a bag of chips and a banana from the supply drawer for Zazu, he heard Jamie say for the second time to the same customer, "How's your day going?" Never mind that at nine in the morning, most people hadn't experienced enough of the day to assess it fairly.

Though it was hard to believe that only an hour had passed from when Drew had first unpeeled Renata's Post-it from the toaster. "Pls look after Zazu": how casually he'd processed those words. He hadn't even paused, taking the bag of coffee from the fridge, shaking grounds into the paper filter.

"What's up with you? You seem super jumpy," Jamie said.

"I'm fine," Drew said, though nothing in his life seemed less true. His eyes were trained at the end of the lobby, the ladies' room door. In his frenzy to assemble snacks, he'd missed seeing Zazu walk in. Had she emerged? He looked out the window, but she wasn't anywhere near his car. "Has Susan come in yet?"

Jamie shook her head, making the puckering face that the word "Susan" invoked among all her staff. "Not yet." She continued looking at Drew with her sleepy, half-mast eyes. Her eyeliner was smudged, making Drew think of the black greasepaint he and his teammates had smeared under their eyes before football games. He felt a sudden wave of nostalgia for those days—only four years ago! His mother in the bleachers, veiny hands clenched, twisting them in that nervous way she did—that made his stomach hurt.

"You really okay? Can I take off?"

Drew felt an almost superstitious reluctance to say yes. As long as Jamie was here, in her rumpled dress, a box of Tic Tacs clutched in her hand, the future was still remote.

"I told my girlfriend my mother is dead," Drew said then.

He and Renata had been at The Oasis, in fact, when he'd said it. He'd snuck Renata into a vacant room on one of his days off. Zazu had been at preschool. Renata loved fucking in hotel rooms for the same reason she loved eating out: because someone else had to clean up the mess.

"But she's not dead. And you want to know why I did it?"

Jamie narrowed her eyes.

"I thought it was less hassle that way. Ever since I can remember, I've done stupid shit because it seemed easier at the time."

It was true that the prospect of his mother and Renata converging seemed anything but easy. He pictured Renata as a cue ball, his mother the other fifteen balls racked together into a fragile mass that would be no match for the cue ball's break shot.

But he'd also instinctively understood that Renata would like him less if she knew he had a mother, and an uber-protective one at that. Renata complained about how cushy so many kids had it—mothers always around to pick up after them, bake cakes for their birthdays, accommodate their egg allergies, sew labels into their sweaters. They were doomed to grow up soft, dependent. Spineless, she'd said, and he'd pictured that Portuguese man-of-war—a soft, spineless creature, yes, but hardly delicate.

Renata once contrasted Zazu's preschool friends to some kids she'd seen in a documentary: five-year-olds from a village in Ghana, building and tending their own fires. She'd described those kids cooking meat wrapped in banana leaves while their parents farmed, and Drew had understood at that moment the story Renata told herself. Neglect was her parenting skill.

So what was Drew's story then? Whose mother had sewed labels in everything he owned, including his underwear, so the kids at summer camp called him "Andrew Wilson Huckaby"? She'd only allowed him to attend because he'd promised to call her every night before bed and because he'd promised that if he felt at all unsafe he'd work the word "airship" into one of his sentences. A "safe word" she had called it, the word chosen because of the unlikeliness of him uttering it by accident. But the word had hovered in his head, multiplied, like vultures over a carcass. He'd whispered it under his breath all month long. Imagined the word leaving his lips like rings of smoke from the blue caterpillar's mouth in *Alice in Wonderland*, only like the Hindenburg, the word ignited and crashed.

Drew had been the only sober adult in the house when Renata had brought up those kids from the documentary, and he'd noticed Zazu's pink cheeks that evening, felt her warm forehead. Still, as soon as he'd given Zazu some ibuprofen and tucked her into bed, he'd gotten so high that later that night, he'd tried to order pizza by punching buttons on the TV remote. He and Renata had fallen asleep naked on the living room floor, her nipple like a pacifier in his mouth.

When Zazu emerged from the hotel bathroom, Drew didn't notice her. She might have made it all the way out to the car if it hadn't been for Jamie. She called "Hey, Honey!" to the little girl in front of the automatic doors, a paper doll silhouetted against the bright outside, and asked her where she'd come from and where she was going.

Drew was too busy wondering if Renata had left for good and what the heck he was going to do if she had. Picturing calling his mother, the way she would loop the phone cord around her wrist while he explained about the four-year-old on his hands. Regurgitating the word airship, airship, airship.

AMUSE-BOUCHES

STEPHANIE

My cousin Stephanie, only four months older than me but always the first to do everything, has a boyfriend. This boyfriend lives in a neighborhood so lush and green that when she walks the sidewalks with Roy at night, most of the street asleep, the two of them passing a cigarette back and forth (she's the first to smoke too), she says she imagines she and her boyfriend are lightning bugs in a forest. "Or it's like I'm Alice when she shrinks to the size of a flower," Stephanie says, "Remember? All those bitchy flowers think she's a weed." She tells me this on Easter at our grandmother's house. She's snuck some of Uncle Nick's Crown Royal into our lemonade, and we're swinging on the porch, biting the heads off Peeps. Only the yellow chicks, because the other colors are unnatural. Of course, the yellow isn't natural either, but the illusion of naturalness makes a difference, according to Stephanie. The yellow chicks taste better. "It's like Astroturf," she says. "Who wants to run around on Astroturf that's any color but green?"

UNCLE NICK

Uncle Nick is a district manager at Safeway, and he tells us that the groceries in the low-income neighborhoods (neither lush nor particularly green) sell three times as much cat food. "Do you want to know why?" he says. "Lots of elderly people live in those neighborhoods, people on fixed incomes." Uncle Nick always tells stories this way, in stages, waiting for comments. I picture an old lady with a silver-blue bun at the nape of her neck. She's stroking one of those masked cats that looks like a raccoon, while another cat slip-knots around her legs. "Old people like cats?" I say. Stephanie laughs like I've said the funniest thing. Uncle Nick shakes his head and says, "Cheap protein." "Oh Nick, not at dinner," says my aunt Nancy, and then, "Pass the stuffing, please."

MR. FIELDING

I set a leaf of lettuce and a three-legged cricket before an iridescent green beetle I scooped up off the straw doormat. The beetle had been on its back in the center of the "O" in "Welcome," his elegant little legs, like the intricately carved neck of my violin, wriggling. He reminds me of a passenger in an innertube floating down a lazy river. I'm trying to figure out what the beetle eats. Behind me, my friends Jules and Tara talk about boys and sugar and Mr. Fielding, our biology teacher. *Martin's lips are so soft. Carlos's dimples kill me. I'd fuck him. You don't even know what that means. That espresso chip gelato, that's what his kisses taste like. Ian is so hot for you. Like chocolate buttercream frosting, that's what I bet Mr. Fielding tastes like. Mr. Fielding can dissect me anytime. Girl, give me some of those jelly beans now or I'll tell him you said that.* The beetle refuses my offerings, scuttles away.

ROY

Stephanie's phone dings. We're watching *The Great British Baking Show*, but Stephanie is in the bathroom. She keeps checking the zit on her chin. Prom is Saturday; she's in despair. "It looks like a wart. I look like a witch." Her boyfriend Roy is a senior. She's the only girl in her freshman class going to prom. Her phone dings again, and I read the text from Roy. "Can't stop thinking about last night. I want to eat you again." Eat her? I think of ogres, which makes me think of Shrek, which makes me wish that we were six again and arguing about who got to be dumpy Princess Fiona, legs like green drumsticks.

JULES

Jules's parents make donuts every Sunday morning, punching out the center of Pillsbury biscuit dough discs with a soda cap. I've never seen so much oil in my life. The biscuit dough swims in it, turns brown, and then it's off to roll around in cinnamon-and-sugar sand. Jules says, "Ugh. Please tell me we have yogurt in the fridge." I eat two donuts and four holes. I stop only because Jules is eyeing me the way she does Tara when Tara drips vinegar onto her French fries. I wonder when Jules stopped eating donuts. We used to wear them around our fingers like engagement rings. In a single morning we'd go through four marriages apiece.

MOM

When Mom runs over a rabbit on the way to the grocery store, she screams, pulls to the side of the road. I open the car door. "What are you doing?" she says. "I'm going to go look at it. Why else did you stop?" I say. "Because I'm too stressed to drive. I need to catch my breath," she says. I leave her in the car, her palm against her sternum like she's holding it in place until glue sets. The way the rabbit's legs twitch makes me think of Tim Southward, who lived next door to us up until I started fifth grade. He used to twitch too, his whole torso, like he was being zapped with tiny bolts of electricity. When I get back in the car, Mom says, "Sometimes I don't know about you."

JULES

"Would you rather be a predator or a prey?" Jules asks. We've been playing "Would you rather" since we met in sixth grade. Jules will ask, "Would you rather have a rhinoceros horn in the middle of your forehead, or really itchy genitals?" There's a pattern to her would-you-rathers: one option is always some kind of humiliating public spectacle, like the horn, or foot-long nose hair; one is hidden, but excruciating. Always, I end up choosing the hidden problem. But now I tell her, "That's loaded phrasing: 'predator' and 'prey.' If you'd asked, would I rather be a carnivore or an herbivore, I'd pick herbivore, because being a carnivore would be gross—blood sticking to your fur and flies bugging you. But no sane person is going to pick 'prey' over 'predator.'" Jules shakes her head. "I disagree. Think about it: a predator's whole life is scheming for the next meal, always on the hunt. A prey can just quietly mind her own business and eat grass. She never has to stress about food. And when she gets killed, it's so sudden, a chomp to the neck. I bet she doesn't even know what bit her."

MADAME KAWECKI

In French class, we make macarons. I try to pipe the batter into perfect round discs, but my cookies look more like amoebas with multiple pseudopods. And they are tiny. Ms. Kawecki says, "Ils sont petits!" Then she says that my cookies are bite-sized, like amuse-bouches. When Ms. Kawecki took us to a French restaurant a few months earlier, the waiter described the amuse-bouches in great detail, listing every ingredient. When Tara asked Ms. Kawecki why, she said, "Les allergies allimentaires sont très sérieux!" and then asked in English, which she almost never speaks to us, if any of us had any food allergies.

ROY

School has been out one week, and Stephanie is in a coma in the hospital. She'd been out walking with that boyfriend of hers again, and a tree limb fell. Struck her in the head. A freak accident. Roy visits while I'm there. He brings a vase of sunflowers. I lie and say that I was just about to go eat lunch. I'm no good at talking to boys. Plus, I figure he wants to be alone with Stephanie. But as soon as I say, "I'm going to go eat," I think of his text, and I blush. Jules told me what it means. She has an older sister.

LINCOLN

Mom spends all day cooking for Uncle Nick and Aunt Nancy: a lasagna, a pan of chicken verde enchiladas, and two loaves of zucchini bread. In between steps, she taps the counter nervously. I think of how I used to pretend to play piano, dancing my fingers back and forth across Mom's desk. No room for a real piano in our house, though, hence violin lessons. I suck at the violin, like I suck at everything. Even Stephanie's little sister Gretchen is better than me, and she's only eleven. Then there's our cousin Lincoln, who at ten already knows he wants to be an engineer when he grows up. For Grandma Paula's birthday, he built her a marble chute.

TRACY THE TAKER

My fortune cookie at Shanghai Palace last month said, "There are makers, and there are takers." That made Stephanie laugh and laugh. "Tracy the Taker," she called me. That night I had a dream that the world was divided. The Makers had long blue cloaks and glass beads around their throats; the Takers' faces were covered in crumbs. They ate like animals, without using their hands. Stephanie had a dab of plum sauce on her chin at Shanghai Palace, from the Moo shu pork. I didn't tell her about it because she was being such a bitch. Now, in my imagination, I hand her napkin after napkin.

STEPHANIE

It's good to talk to people in comas. I don't know if that's real information, or something I saw on *Grey's Anatomy*. I feel too stupid doing it in front of other people, but when Aunt Nancy goes to the cafeteria to get coffee, I hold Stephanie's hand. "I can't believe all Roy has is a scratch on his arm. He didn't even need stitches," I tell her. "I bet all the girls from your school feel so sorry for him." But that trajectory sounds too negative. Why would Stephanie want to return to a world where injuries are so arbitrarily divvied? What will make her want to open her eyes? So I take a breath, and then I start reciting to her all the foods she most likes to eat, everything delicious waiting if only she surfaces.

Cadbury eggs with the sticky filling, triple-cream cheese, fried calamari. Pickled green beans from Uncle Nick's Bloody Mary. The first spring plums. Pistachios that dye our fingertips red. Food that requires effort: the soft heart of an artichoke; pomegranates that Steph will only eat after she's peeled away every last thin bit of skin.

RULE OF THUMB

ELLEN'S MOTHER TELLS HER STORIES THAT make women look imperiled and men depraved, like about the origin of the phrase, "rule of thumb." According to Ellen's mother, it derives from a colonial statute that men weren't allowed to beat their wives with a rod thicker than their thumb. "Let's hope those Puritans weren't like your father," she said. "That man has Kosher pickles for thumbs."

And that "pleased as punch" originates from Punch and Judy puppet shows, in which the brute Punch beat, and often murdered, both his baby and wife, and then laughed maniacally.

Not all of Ellen's mother's stories are about language, however. For instance, she's convinced that her younger sister Linda's husband Dave is a pedophile. She warns Ellen and Patricia to stay far away from him. "Don't even let him hug you today," her mother says. "Put your hand out and shake instead. Then promptly scrub that hand with hot water and soap."

Today is Ellen's older cousin Harriet's wedding. Ellen has invited her girlfriend, Patricia. Not that Ellen's mother knows that the girls make out in Ellen's bedroom when Patricia comes over. One might think Ellen's mother would be relieved her daughter is into girls. Patricia says, "Your mother thinks I'm awesome!" But Ellen knows her mother's affection would immediately evaporate if she knew the real state of things. No more her mother playing Boggle with them and complimenting Patricia on all her four- and five-letter words, no more giving Patricia needlepoint lessons, no more telling Patricia she's a good influence on Ellen: just look at how much more organized Ellen's room is, thanks to Patricia rubbing off on her.

Her mother's warnings, Ellen has decided, are less about men than about sex. Ellen remembers too well the first time her mother talked to her about sex. This was part of a month-long ordeal in which Ellen, then six or seven, had to suffer through her mother reading to her nightly from an encyclopedic book that covered every embarrassing topic concerning being human. Some of the graphics were meticulously detailed, such as the sperms' travels through the uterus, the muscled organ striated like the old-fashioned hard candies Ellen's grandmother kept in a glass bowl on her coffee table. In contrast, the graphic about the act of sex was puzzlingly vague: a cartoon man and woman wrapped in a patchwork quilt, a red heart rising from their mutual gaze like a bubble from a soap bottle. Of this picture, her mother said, "Sex is supposed to mean when a man and a woman who love each other press together and touch each other lovingly; but sadly, sometimes the love part is missing."

Odd that a woman so jaded about romance is such a leaking faucet at weddings, but such is the case. Ellen's mother is wearing waterproof mascara and has stuffed Kleenex into her purple leather purse. "I have plenty if you girls need any," she tells them in the car.

Ellen's father, who is driving, says, "I thought you said Harriet's fiancé is milquetoast."

Ellen's mother says, "He is. I did. Crying at weddings is just an involuntary response, like hiccupping."

Patricia squeezes Ellen's thigh then. After they arrive and Ellen pulls her away to tell her to be more careful, Patricia says, "Touching you is an involuntary response."

Ellen says, "If you were a guy, that would be a very rapey thing to say."

She expects a laugh, but Patricia looks stony. "Sometimes I think you wish I were a guy."

"What? That makes no sense," Ellen says. After all, Patricia is the one who dated Tom Callahan for nearly a year. The closest Ellen has ever come to having a boyfriend is when she let Anthony Grigg pet her hair at one of Erin Joyce's movie nights, and Monday at school he presented her with a musk-scented note asking her to go to Olive Garden with him, an offer she politely declined.

But Patricia has already turned in a huff and is walking towards the church. Her sleeveless dress exposes a creamy wedge of back.

Patricia's moods unnerve Ellen, the sudden way she takes umbrage. Her enthusiasms are violent but fleeting. One month she's obsessed with mochi balls, then it's Mae West movies, then it's Sylvia Plath, then it's bacon on everything: bacon bits on donuts, bacon ice cream at that weird, pretentious ice-cream store around the corner from Patricia's house that has flavors like Olive Oil and Pepper 'n Salt. Ellen worries that it will be the same with this queer girl gambit. Now Patricia might be baking lemon bars for the Gay-Straight Alliance, wearing an enamel rainbow ring, and insisting that she and Ellen go to prom together, but next week Ellen may have gone the way of bacon ice cream: another discarded appetite.

Inside the church, Ellen finds Patricia in one of the back pews, laughing with a girl whose bright red lips contrast the girlish French braids in her hair. Patricia doesn't see Ellen standing at the church's entrance, or maybe she merely pretends.

The stained-glass window nearest Patricia shows a half-naked man and woman, their skin gray, standing shoulder to shoulder before God and what Ellen assumes is supposed to be a tree, though it looks more like the diagram in her freshman biology textbook of a hair follicle, the bulbous part pointed up. The man's hands are palms together. He smiles piously at God. The woman's eyes are downcast, while her finger points at the man. Even to Ellen she looks guilty. That's the point, her mother would say. These stories were written by men to justify the oppression of women.

"Your dad is going to need a shotgun to keep the boys away," a voice says. Ellen startles. Her Uncle Will, husband of Ellen's mother's second youngest sister, Jackie. Several people turn to look at them, including Patricia and Ellen's mother, who is seated three pews in front of Patricia.

"Har har," Ellen says. Uncle Will looks confused and annoyed: this isn't the way Ellen is supposed to respond. She's supposed to giggle, blush, and stare at her feet, like Eve in the painting. And because she's not looking down, she sees her mother frown and shake her head. For all her mother's admonitions about her brothers-in-law specifically and men generally, she's the world's biggest stickler for good manners. Will is meant to be decoded only in absentia. Ellen can already hear her mother, loudly expostulating at home after the reception: "What the heck was that idiotic, violent comment? That man is such a sexist moron. Ellen, do you know what 'shotgun' references?" Then looking over at Ellen's father, laughing—no, chortling. "Damn, Freddy, hard to imagine you with a shotgun. That's hilarious." The whole imaginary scene unreels before Ellen, zooming in on her father's face, pink and exhausted, studying the chicken on his plate as if it will finally reveal to him the kind of man his wife requires him to be.

Uncle Will excuses himself, supposedly to find Ellen's Aunt Jackie, but his eyes are on Patricia, or maybe her Lolita look-alike companion.

Ellen's mother, though not religious, has said a dozen times that she thanks God that Jackie and Will don't have kids. She claims that if he had a daughter, he'd probably be like her co-worker Don, the guy infamous for the incestuous Christmas card featuring a photo of him and his then twelve-year-old daughter looking like they were posing for a school dance. She was sitting in his lap, his arm circled her waist. She looked at her father, Ellen thought, like she was hoping for him to make a move.

Not unlike Lolita seems to be looking at Patricia now, right here in front of Ellen's extended family, and in a church of all places.

Screw this, Ellen thinks, and slides into the pew next to Patricia. Before Patricia can give her a dirty look, Ellen puts her arm around her. "Hello," Ellen says to the Lolita. Up close she sees a spray of acne, like breadcrumbs, on the girl's rosy cheeks. "I'm Ellen."

"Carrie," says the girl, looking startled. Her round, hazel eyes remind Ellen of tortoiseshell buttons. Patricia looks startled too, and then pleased. Patricia's smile is Ellen's favorite thing about her: it converts her from pretty blonde to something lupine and predatory.

Patricia has been bugging Ellen for weeks to be more demonstrative. "Stop pretending," she said. But Ellen can picture, with the same zoom-in clarity she can picture her father's Eve-like, downcast face, receiving Christmas cards years and years from now featuring Patricia, her handsome husband, and their blond kids, on a sailboat, wearing forest green Fair Isle sweaters.

Under her fingers Ellen feels the crunchy strap of Patricia's dress, her warm shoulder. Around her she feels eyes. It's like that scene where Snow White is running through the woods, and all around her hover blinking, yellow eyes. In physics class, they've been learning about the observer effect, the fact that observation doesn't happen in a vacuum: simply by looking at something, we shape the characteristics of the object we see. Like how you can't check the pressure in automobile tires without letting out some measure of air.

Would her mother be paranoid and prickly if she'd grown up surrounded by less creepy, lecherous men? Ellen remembers Uncle Will, saying of her cousin Marianne, the one her age, "Marianne, you're really growing up." Will's leer, Marianne defensively crossing her arms.

Though the scrutiny of all the female relatives has been just as bad. Her Aunt Gretchen nicknamed Marianne's sister Harriet "Hairy." Ellen remembers the first time she saw Harriet wearing a bleaching strip on her upper lip. Harriet had looked like a photo negative Hitler: small white moustache instead of black.

These same eyes on Ellen now, the gesture of Ellen's arm

around Patricia feels performative and awkward. Ellen's mother looks at her the way she did when Ellen was going through that *Desperately Seeking Susan* Madonna phase and came down the stairs for school with her hair curly as a poodle's.

Carrie resumes telling Patricia about her mother's resolution the previous year to not buy any new clothes or shoes for a year. Carrie recalls the tribulations, how one day her mother would feel her wardrobe was in shambles because she didn't own the right kind of jeans. Then the next she'd think the problem was that she owned too many jeans. "Desire is a fickle thing," Carrie says, more to Patricia than to Ellen.

"Oh, I know," Patricia says. To both Ellen's relief and consternation, Patricia pulls free of Ellen's embrace. She shows Carrie the tattoo that circles her left arm, a quote from Sylvia Plath: "Perhaps when we find ourselves wanting everything, it is because we are dangerously close to wanting nothing."

According to Marianne, Harriet was only marrying Charlie because she was afraid no one else would ever ask her. "She's got like this crazy phobia about dying alone in a bathtub," Marianne said, as they drank shots of vodka from Aunt Gretchen's not-so-secret stash in the laundry room, behind the fabric softener. "With Charlie around, if she does die in a bathtub, he can dress her before the paramedics show."

That and the gifts, Marianne had said. Harriet had been checking her registries these last several months with the same frequency that she checks her social media accounts. Tallying what had been purchased, what remained. Fretting about the choices she'd made: Was $180 for a meat cleaver excessive? Would she even enjoy sleeping on silk sheets?

Ellen remembers asking her mother a long time ago how she knew she wanted to marry Ellen's father. Her mother had seemed perplexed by the question. "No one ever really knows what they want."

MY COWORKER ALDONA

to her apartment for refreshments (her word) and a movie for the fourth time in two weeks, I reluctantly said yes.

Aldona and I work in the women's locker room at the university's older gym. We hand out clean towels to naked women, most of them 40+. The students prefer the newer gym where Lady Gaga and Beyoncé roar from the speakers. Aldona and I are thankful that we work in the older gym, but that's where our commonalities end. She's twelve years my senior, a grad student in psychology, a smoker, and she's Lithuanian.

The stench of cigarettes in Aldona's apartment is so thick that the shortbread cookies she has arranged in a spiral on a white plate taste like ashes.

On the screen, a young woman staggers through an empty hallway. Her breathing is ragged, her cheeks are streaked with mascara. She opens one door, then another, apparently unable to decide where to hide.

The inability to make decisions indicates that you have not

accepted yourself as an independent individual, Aldona said the other day when we were folding the gym's scratchy towels.

This was after the third time I'd turned down her offer to come over. "Sorry, I have plans," I said, and Aldona folded four towels in silence and then offered up this pronouncement on indecisiveness. There was no obvious correlation between my comment and hers. It wasn't as if I were dithering. I'd been if anything too forceful. Still, I flushed.

I always pictured therapists as refusing to express their opinions, parrying any question with their own ("What do *you* think about that conversation with your mother?"). Aldona struck me as weirdly judgmental for someone planning to be a psychologist. Now, watching the terrified woman on the screen flutter and swoop between doorways, I think of all the terrible things I could say to Aldona: underneath the cigarettes, she smells meaty, as though she's been churning out sausages from her mouth; one of the hairs on the bottom of her chin looks almost pubic; and only a creep invites her coworker over to watch a movie when the one television in her apartment is in her tiny bedroom, so they have to take up opposite sides of her double bed, sides that are not separated by a wide enough chasm. I am leaning so far toward the edge of what has become my side of Aldona's bed that I'm like a boulder on a precipice, flirting with gravity.

For a would-be psychologist, Aldona has no intuition at all.

Do I chalk up her crazy obtuseness to a language barrier?

Aldona sometimes sprinkles articles where they aren't needed, excludes them where they are, like a Cockney with the letter H. Or maybe Aldona is conducting some bizarre experiment to locate my breaking point. What will it take to make me scream like the woman on the screen, her eyes so wide open her irises are encased by white?

"Mind if I open your window?" I cough a few times for emphasis.

Aldona takes a drag from her cigarette, exhales slowly.

She says, "'Why is this happening to me?' is unanswerable question. The appropriate question is, why I allow this to happen to me? Or better: why I cause this to happen to me?"

I resist the urge to smash the plate of cookies over Aldona's head. Instead, I get up and open the window. It's humid, the peak of summer, but still I press my face into the mesh screen. I suck in hot air. It's like being in the locker room when the showers are running.

A boy riding by on his bicycle stops and dismounts. He yanks down his shorts and moons me. Before I blink, his shorts are back in place, and he's pedaling away.

I open my mouth to tell Aldona what just happened—she's the only person here—but as I turn toward her, a machete slices through the movie heroine's skull as smoothly as though through a block of cheese.

Aldona nods, taps ashes into the hollow body of a ceramic mouse.

IT WAS STAPLED TO THE CHICKEN

Stefan's and my school gets out twenty minutes earlier than our sister school down the block, Immaculate Conception—or, as Stefan and I call it, Ejaculate Conception. We sit on the low brick wall opposite the entrance and share a cigarette as we wait for Rose and Geraldine to emerge from seventh period Chemistry. Rose is Stefan's, Geri is mine. Geri is prettier, especially her lips, which are puffy and remind me of knuckles; Rose has better boobs and, if Stefan is telling the truth, she also likes giving him blowjobs. Once she licked his dick in the mall family bathroom as casually as she might a mint chip ice-cream cone.

From this distance, when Ejaculate Conception's student body emerges from the building—which sort of resembles a skull, the doors the mouth—you can imagine the crowd of girls in tan, pleated skirts and white shirts are maggots spilling out of roadkill.

Our girls slowly take shape as they approach. Rose and Geri are the same height, and both have long, brown hair. So I can't tell them apart when they first veer from the swarm. I think of the brine shrimp we grew in biology the year before—how first they were tiny ripples in the water. Then a week later, we could make out their strange, feathery bodies.

When the girls are finally close enough to touch, something weird happens. Geri doesn't even look at me. She makes straight for Stefan. Plants her lips on his. Stefan grabs hold of her hips.

Before I can protest, Rose puts her arms around me. "Miss me?" she says. She smells like honeysuckle, just like Geri. Against my chest I feel the soft press of her breasts.

I try to catch Stefan's eye but he's too busy kissing Geri. When she finally leans away, she says, "Your place, Babe?"

Geri has never, not once, called me Babe. Dumbass, from time to time. She's affectionate but not sentimental; it's as if the only endearments that can come from those knuckle lips are soft punches.

"*Mais oui, ma chérie*," Stefan says. He takes Geri's hand, and they walk, arms swinging.

I'm waiting for someone to laugh and say, "Gotcha!" But what Rose says is "I've got a new one for you."

"What?" I say.

"What's the difference between a baby and an onion?"

I say, "Is this some kind of a joke?"

Dead baby jokes are Geri's shtick.

"Of course, it's a joke," she says. "Give up? No one cries when you chop up the baby!" She grins.

Then she groans and yanks me to my feet. "You're acting weird. What's up?"

I say, "I haven't the slightest clue."

Ever since Stefan told me about Rose's penchant for blowjobs, I've been thinking about the randomness of relationships. For instance, if Stefan and I hadn't gone to the arcade that Saturday afternoon in October, we might never have met Rose and Geri. Or if Rose hadn't had that swollen pimple symmetrically situated in the center of her chin that day, I might have deliberated more over which girl I preferred. It's crazy how a moment's choice can determine whether five months later you're the lucky beneficiary of blowjobs in mall bathrooms, or you're with the girl who keeps saying "I'm not ready."

When my mom married my step-dad, Isaac, she said, "He's the love of my life," as though she hadn't said the same thing once about my dad. As if at the age of thirty-six, having known Isaac for less than two years, she could possibly have a long view shot of her whole life.

We follow Stefan and Geri, now yards ahead of us. Stefan's place is always the preferred location, because his mother stocks the pantry with cinnamon Pop-Tarts and Kettle Sea Salt & Vinegar chips, and because Stefan's parents both work. With my thumb, I rub Rose's thin gold ring, her grandmother's wedding ring, which Stefan has said creeps him out, like Rose is betrothed to her corpse grandfather. On her wrist is the baby blue Swatch Stefan gave her for Christmas. I helped him pick it out.

In the kitchen, Geri says, "I'm starving."

When Stefan opens the pantry, she shoves him inside and pulls the door closed behind them. I hear laughter. Then I hear bodies slamming around, cans and boxes hitting the floor.

Rose says, "You're hurting my hand."

My fingernails have made impressions on her skin. The dents look like teeth marks, like a small animal has been nibbling her.

I think of a story my cousin Alex told me. He was going out with an identical twin, a girl named Maura. His friend Louis dated her sister Rebecca. And sometimes, the twins would switch.

We were stoned when Alex told me this story. We were lying on his double bed, looking at the ceiling, where years ago Alex and I had glued a spiral of glow-in-the-dark stars. He wasn't exactly sure when the girls started impersonating each other, he said. He may have missed it initially. But one day, he was making out with Maura, and suddenly he knew she was Rebecca.

"How'd you know?" I asked.

"It was just a feeling. I had my eyes closed, and I opened them and gave her a look. The way she looked back at me was freaky. She knew that I knew. But I didn't say anything, and we kept making out."

"Are you sure?"

"Of course! Anyway, soon enough I confirmed it. Becca still had her appendix; she didn't have Maura's scar. That scar kind of disgusted me, to tell the truth. It looked like a fat, pink cat-erpillar. They used to switch maybe once a week. I don't know if Louis ever figured it out, though I guess he must have, given Maura's scar. We never talked about it. Like the four of us had an unspoken agreement."

"You didn't even talk to Maura about it?"

"Dude, why the hell would I?"

What I felt, hearing the story a year ago, was wonder and envy. This was before I started going out with Geri, and two girls seemed like a crazy surfeit of riches. I never wondered if Alex minded that, while he was banging the one sister, maybe on that very bed, under that whorl of pale green stars, his girlfriend was behind another closed door with his friend. Or that the sisters were making their own comparisons.

This situation is similar, except, of course, for one crucial dif-ference—Geri and Rose aren't identical. True, Stefan's Chinese aunt couldn't keep the girls straight when she visited a few weeks ago, but that was a race thing, like how Stefan kept confusing the two black superheroes, Falcon and War Machine, in *Captain America: Civil War*.

I'm like goddamn Dorothy in *The Wizard of Oz*.

I decide the best course of action is to mimic my cousin Alex and play along. After all, haven't I always wondered what it would be like to cup Rose's breasts? So I lift Rose's hand to my lips and kiss the indentations I made with my nails. Then I kiss her neck. When I finally put my hand to her breast, I half expect her to slap me, but she doesn't. Not even. She fucking moans.

And here's another weird thing: I expect that touching Rose's breasts will feel wrong, dangerous even. Like when I stole a whole chicken fryer from the grocery store, hid it inside my leather jacket, because Stefan and I were playing a game: Winner is the guy who manages to steal the most conspicuous item. But after that moan, I don't think about anything other than how good Rose feels, how her breast fills my whole palm. In fact, I don't even realize that Stefan and Geri have come out of the pantry until Geri bangs a wooden spoon against the bottom of one of Stefan's parents' pots.

Rose and I both yell, "Fuck!" at the same time.

Stefan and Geri laugh. Then Stefan says, "We're going up to my room. See you in like an hour?" He winks.

"Wait, what?" I look at Geri. The last time she called me Dumbass was a few days earlier when I tried to slip my finger inside her. "What did I tell you about that, Dumbass? I'm not ready."

She looks back at me, waves, and says, "Later, Gator." Which is not the kind of thing Geri ever says; it's Rose who likes cornball rhymes, Rose who says, "In a while, Crocodile."

Enough is enough, I think, and I grab Geri's arm. When she whirls around, not only is she not smiling, not finally letting the air out of this fucked up prank; she's looking at me like she's scared of me.

"What the hell?" Stefan says. He looks like he wants to punch me.

And Rose looks like she might cry.

I picture the ceiling in Alex's bedroom, the glow-in-the-dark stars I helped him stick there when he was ten and I was eight. He didn't want them scattered; he had a very precise spiral shape in mind. I said to him, "But that isn't what space looks like." I wanted to put up the Big Dipper, or Orion's Belt.

But Alex said, "I don't care about what's really there. I want to build my own universe." I couldn't explain why I found that so unsettling. Partly it was the spiral shape itself, the whirlpool way it sucked me in.

Last Saturday Stefan and I and the girls watched a movie in his basement, Hitchcock's *Vertigo*. There's a scene where Jimmy Stewart dreams he's falling into an open grave. At the bottom of this long, rabbit hole of a descent is a rotating spiral. That whole movie freaked me out, but that scene most of all. "Shit," I said.

Geri laughed and kissed my neck. She said, "Open your eyes. It's over."

That's what I want to happen now: for Geri to throw her arms around me, call me Dumbass or whatever the fuck she wants to call me. I want her to say that order in the universe has been restored.

I want Stefan to bust out laughing and say, like I did when I managed to smuggle that whole chicken out into the parking lot, "Guess who's the motherfucking champion now?!"

Instead, Geri twists out of my grip. Stefan glares at me. Rose says, "What the hell was that?"

I feel like the subject of an experiment, like a brine shrimp swimming around in a plastic tank of water while my closest friends pour in kerosene and watch me flounder.

If Alex were here, he'd say, "You get to make out with Rose, Idiot! The blowjob enthusiast, remember? What the fuck are you squabbling about?"

I take a deep breath. Then I laugh. To all three of them, I say, "I was just screwing with you guys."

Stefan narrows his eyes at me. Then he and Geri head upstairs.

Rose says, "Not funny."

I close my eyes and kiss her.

Soon, Rose relaxes. I do, too. She takes my hand and leads me to Stefan's basement. She pushes me down against the couch and climbs on top of me. I put my hand on her breast. She moans. I'm smiling as I kiss her, because I'm imagining Rose's mouth as a vortex I'm going to plug with my dick. Like fucking Rose's mouth is my ruby red slippers. But when I undo my zipper and grab her hand, she stiffens and pulls up to a sitting position. She says, "Oh shit. I totally forgot to tell you this one. Why did the dead baby cross the road?"

THE PRESENT MOMENT

"THERE IS NO SUCH THING AS THE PRES-
ent," the guy I'm sleeping with says. He tilts my head back as
though my neck is a box he's opening. He traces lines back and
forth along my trachea, like he's looking for an invisible latch.

We're in my tiny apartment kitchen. I've just uncorked the
bottle of red wine he brought, poured our glasses. I've broken so
many wine glasses now that I no longer have a matching pair. His
glass is the large one with the very thin bowl. It's my favorite glass,
but it's safer in his hands.

He says, "I am not the guy you are sleeping with. I am the
guy you have fucked and the guy you will fuck again in the future."

"But this moment," I say. "Your fingers on my skin. You
standing in my kitchen. This is not the past or the future."

He smiles at me like my sister smiles at her little girl, Juney,
when Juney insists something ridiculous, such as when Juney said
she was going to marry their cat and give birth to a litter of half-
cat, half-human babies.

He says, "It's something I heard on a TED talk. I know it

sounds crazy at first, but think about it. As soon as my mouth pronounces a word, that word becomes part of the past."

I notice for the first time that his right eye is slightly smaller than his left eye, like my right breast is smaller than my left breast, and now I'm picturing his eyes as tiny gelatinous breasts, his pupils their smooth, Sharpied-on nipples.

I say, "But during the pronouncing, when your mouth is making the shape of a word, that is a present action."

"Or, to use your other example," I continue, "What if we go to the bedroom right now and start having sex? Then you are not just the guy I have fucked and will fuck. You become the guy I am currently, at this very moment, in the present, fucking. Because otherwise, every nanosecond of fucking is a separate fuck. If we fuck for ten minutes, we'd have to say we fucked a trillion times."

That look of certainty shakes from his face. Watching it drop away, I realize that the reason I am, have been, and maybe will again sleep with the guy I am sleeping with has to do with that expression of assurance. When he first asked me for my number three weeks ago, back at The Lone Palm, he was wearing it. And even though he wasn't really my type (he's lean to the point of angular, and has messy, voluminous hair), I said, "Sure, okay." And he had that same expression the first time we had sex, and I thought, wow, maybe I could fall in love with this guy.

I realize all these things—the existence of that expression, and that it had real significance in the past—only now. It's because I see the confidence that once made him something more desirable than his essential self slip away. It's my own philosophical mini-epiphany. I say, "Whoa."

He says, "Actually, before we fuck, I'd like to drink some of this wine."

I study his formerly-smug-and-now-uncertain face, trying to sort out whether he wants wine because he's now not that into me, or because he has a drinking problem (now that I think about it, every time we've had sex he's been buzzed), or because he knows I've exploded his silly "there is no present" pseudo-philosophy and he's one of those dudes who needs to feel superior to the woman he's sleeping with or, even creepier, because he was gaslighting me, and his claim that "there is no present" was merely the first step in a series of insane falsities that will eventually unhinge my reason and turn me into a madwoman.

I'll grant him this: the present is as elusive as a good man. It's difficult to be in the moment when I'm already seeing what lies ahead.

On the other hand, I recognize this is the moment when I know I am no longer sleeping with, and will not in the future sleep with, the guy I was sleeping with.

COUNTERBALANCES

STEALING MARY'S CAR IS A NEGATIVE feedback loop. We're correcting an imbalance, restoring homeostasis. "Like injecting insulin to uptake excess glucose from the bloodstream of a diabetic," Bernice says as she fishes Mary's car keys from Mary's purse and dangles them from her pinky finger. In Bernice's analogy, Bernice and I are the suffering diabetic, Mary and Liam and Hand the glut of glucose.

I say, "I'm bringing the rabbit."

I don't want to take my hands off the rabbit. It's velvety, the color of a licked caramel.

We've been waiting nearly thirty minutes in these guys' apartment for Mary to descend the stairs from their rooftop. Liam, the hot guy, brought her there, because Mary said, "There's a full moon tonight. I just love a full moon." She traced the lip of her beer bottle with her fingertip. Mary was wearing her tight, expensive jeans. No doubt her ulterior motive, besides getting Liam alone, was to show off her ass climbing the stairs.

Ten minutes ago, the bearded guy with the scarred hand—

somehow neither of us caught his name earlier at the bar—abandoned us to go "check on them."

Always, guys prefer Mary over Bernice and me. Always, Mary is happy to absorb the attention.

As we head out to the car, Bernice says, "What kind of grown men own a fucking rabbit?" She tugs at her skirt. She's been battling that spandex all evening.

Some guy called my house one night—my parents still had a landline. When I answered, he said, "Carly?" Instead of telling him he had the wrong number, I said, "Yeah?" My mouth was full of leftover lasagna. He said, "Carly, what do you have in your mouth?" I listed every ingredient from spinach to fennel to ricotta cheese. He said, "You're so alive, Carly. So fucking alive."

That pretty much sums up how I feel about the rabbit. It's warm, it has the perfect amount of heft, and beneath my fingertips, its muscles twitch. I don't want to let it go.

In the car, Bernice says, "We're going to the beach. Light me a cigarette?"

One hand on the rabbit, I push in the car's electric lighter, though Mary forbids smoking in her car. I see the ocean in the distance. That is, I know the ocean is there because of the absence of lights. Or rather, I trust it's there, that we're not driving instead into the belly of a giant beast, like Han Solo in *The Empire Strikes Back*.

When we reach the seawall, Bernice parks the car near concrete steps leading down to the sand, where three guys play Frisbee in the moonlight.

With the sea breeze, the air is chilly. I tuck the rabbit inside my buttoned cardigan, nestling the animal against my chest. It peers up at me, its nose wriggling in rhythm with its heart.

Bernice shakes her head. "Sometimes you act like you're twelve," she says. "Leave the goddamn rabbit in the car." She motions toward the three guys with her chin.

"I don't want to." I smile at the rabbit. "Anyway, he'll poo everywhere."

"I hope he does," Bernice says. "You saw the way Mary appropriated Liam. Did it matter to her for one second that I saw him first?"

Bernice and I were playing pool when Liam asked if he and Hand could join. I was the one he asked. Bernice was gathering balls from the pockets. Technically, I saw Liam first.

But then Bernice looked up and smiled, and somehow it ended up being Hand who bought me a beer. Though by the time he came back from the bar, Mary had swanned into the room, laughing in that shrill, bedazzling way that turns every straight guy in the room into a bobblehead. Bernice was sulking, and Hand looked back and forth, like he was trying to decide to whom the beer belonged.

The truth is I prefer Hand to Liam, or I would have if only

it weren't for the look of defeat on his face when Mary followed Liam up to the roof. Like they were schoolkids and Liam's mom had packed a Hostess CupCake in his lunchbox, while all Hand got for dessert was a hardened clump of raisins. That look didn't deter Bernice. When Hand came down the hallway holding the rabbit, Bernice feigned interest—pawed at the creature just to have an excuse to stand close to Hand. Maybe that's what he wanted, too, though I don't think so. Because when Bernice said her shoulder ached, an invitation, Hand's response was ibuprofen. He put the rabbit down on the carpet and returned from the bathroom with a 600-count bottle.

Against my stomach, I feel the rabbit's long, silky feet. The way they are both clown-like and elegant reminds me of the pointe shoes Mary, Bernice, and I wore in ballet. I was the best in our class—Queen of the Flowers in our last recital, Mary and Bernice two of the frolicking lambs. Then Mary and Bernice decided that ballet was for kids.

"He's staying with me," I say. I lift the bottom of my sweater, and three pellets fall out.

Bernice freaks. She says, "I was going to say, for the love of God, don't act weird, but it's too late for that."

She pinched me earlier when I asked Hand if he had the makings for a BLT.

"We've got eggs," Hand said. "And peanut butter." He dipped a spoon into the peanut butter and licked it.

"This girl is never not hungry," Bernice said, as though she is the epitome of temperance.

The truth is no body is ever in homeostasis. It's an abstract concept, like infinity. Our anatomy teacher proposed we think of the body's elaborate system of balances as a container full of hourglasses positioned at different angles. When you shift to correct one inequity, you disturb the other balances. Basically, we are all always hungry for something.

Now Bernice hands me the car keys. "I don't have any pockets." She takes off her heels to descend the concrete steps. "You should just stay here. You wouldn't want that rabbit to scamper into the ocean." Then she's like an arrow taking aim at the three guys on the beach.

The rabbit nibbles at one of the buttons on my cardigan, and I remove a carrot from my bag. I took it from the guys' produce drawer. Hand didn't mention they had carrots, maybe because they belonged to the rabbit.

The rabbit eats half a stick and then stops. I eat the rest.

The man calling for Carly telephoned a few more times. He had other questions for Carly: What was she wearing? Was she touching herself?

Carly was always forthcoming. Because the man gave her his undivided attention. Because she imagined the man's breath on her ear as he spoke, his fingers on her thighs.

Mary and Bernice would say that the man on the phone

doesn't count as a real hook-up. He didn't actually touch you, I can hear them say. But what matters is what you feel. I overheard my mom's friend Donna say that when her husband touches her, she feels nothing. On the other hand, brain scans show that the brain responds precisely the same way to an imaginary slice of apple pie as it does to a real slice.

When I reach the sand, the rabbit digs its claws into me. Maybe it's the sound of the tide that has spooked it—like a giant tongue licking the beach.

I finger Mary's car keys. How trusting Bernice is for a girl who just stole her best friend's car.

Then I think of Hand. I wonder if he's getting hungry up on the roof watching Mary flirt with Liam, if he craves another spoonful of peanut butter. Or probably it's the rabbit he longs for—the reliable thump of its tiny heart. Has he returned to the apartment yet and discovered that the two girls he left on the couch have stolen it? I wonder if he knows which girl it was—not the skinny, sulky one, but the quiet one he bought a beer for and then forgot about. Maybe he's remembering what he said to her before he followed Mary up the stairs: "Be careful of that rabbit. He looks harmless, but sometimes he bites."

TWENTY-THREE
SAFETY MANUALS

AFTER THE SPRING SEMESTER OF MY JU-
nior year of college, a semester I spent studying abroad in
Edinburgh, I moved back home for the summer. I was broke
and didn't have anywhere else to go, and the previous summers
I'd gone home, so why not this summer, too? Sure, my seven-
teen-year-old brother, Rod, was a misogynistic asshole and my
parents were miserable and depressing to be around, but I would
live rent-free and save up money for my senior year, and after-
wards I'd never ever spend a night in that house again. Because
I had an aunt who was a senior manager in HR at University
of Texas Medical Branch in Galveston, I was able to get a job
in Radiation & Occupational Safety as an office assistant. It was
nothing glamorous, but it meant not having to wait tables again,
which gave me terrible anxiety, and not having to drive all over
town lying to potential employers like I had previous summers,
pretending I wasn't a college student who would take off in a couple of months.

The office had a receptionist, so I rarely had to answer phones, another task that gave me anxiety. Mostly I copyedited various manuals that needed to be updated: Laser Safety, Radiation Safety, MRI Safety, Fire Safety, X-ray Safety, and so on. There are endless ways to hurt yourself in a hospital.

Galveston was so horrifically hot and humid in the summer and my designated parking area such a far walk from the building where I worked that by the time I entered the air-conditioned office, my skin was slick with sweat, my work blouse sticking to my torso. My first stop after dumping my bag at my desk was the bathroom to blot the oil off my face. Still, I was twenty-one and relatively attractive, an observation I can make easily now but wasn't so confident about back then. The only other woman in the office was the receptionist, Tammy, who was thirty years older than me and the kind of woman who tried so hard to turn heads that in her presence, I felt embarrassed to be female. This is to say that despite how sweaty I may have been, I got a lot of unsolicited attention from men who wandered in and out of the office.

"Hey, Banana," Archie would greet me every day, because he'd caught me the morning I met him eating a banana—I'd overslept and dashed out of the house carrying my breakfast. I say "caught me" as if there is anything wrong with eating food in the workplace, but that's how Archie made me feel. There was a kind of obscene way he said "Banana" that made me want to run out the door.

"Morning, Archie," Tammy would say, and then glare at me,

for being rude (or maybe for being young and pretty). I'd respond, invariably, to those two modes of social coercion, and those two pairs of eyes scrutinizing me, by mumbling, belatedly, "Hi."

The safety manuals I was copyediting made me think about words and phrases in a hyper-attentive, peculiar way. I had a blue pen for making edits and stacks and stacks of sticky notes, and after Archie interrupted me with his smirking "Hey Bananas" and Tammy would unload on me her disciplinary glares, I would find sometimes random phrases I'd scrawled onto my sticky notes, like "asking for it."

Frequently I wondered what would come of the edits I was making. Would they really make their way into a finished product? Did anybody in that office care about commas and colons and subject-verb agreement?

When Dan, the program director, handed me those manuals on the first day, he said, "We've never had the time or the resources to clean these up."

The men in that office kept busy cleaning up more serious messes than stray commas. Archie, for example, was a Senior Radiation Safety Specialist. He and Eduardo trained hospital staff in how to manage all things radiation. Also, they picked up and delivered things radiation-related. When I heard one of them say, "I'm going to go pick up a package," I understood that "package" meant radioactive. What they did with these packages, I didn't know. There was a set of heavy-duty, serious-looking doors in the office that only Archie and Eduardo entered. Bryce, Adesh, and Nolan were occupational safety and fire prevention technicians, and Frank's nametag read "Consultant & Registered Professional Sanitarian." I had even less of a grasp on what those four did exactly, but I knew that many of the "important phone numbers" listed in manuals and printed on the wall of the office, went to them—numbers for biological spills, chemical spills, wet or slippery floors, physical hazards, needlestick-blood-borne pathogen exposure, and so on.

Every Friday, Archie brought donuts into the office, and as the men shoved sticky chocolate-glazed, confetti-sprinkled donuts into their mouths, I thought about what else those hands came into contact with day in and day out and felt a little sick. When Archie pushed the box towards me, I'd shake my head. Then he'd say, "You don't need to diet, Banana. Give in. Take pleasure where you can get it." As he said this, I'd watch Tammy out of the corner of my eye cutting her cinnamon-sugar donut into little bite-sized pieces with plastic utensils.

It was on one of those Donut Fridays, however, that I met Leonard. Leonard was another Registered Professional Sanitarian. He'd been on vacation when I started working in the office and returned the end of my second week. What made me notice him was he didn't look at me the way the other men in the office did—like I was something edible. He looked at me then looked away; his gaze a warm flick. Leonard had ears that stuck out like cup handles, and a strangely long neck that made me think of Balanchine's ballet dancers. But he also had beautiful dark brown eyes with eyelashes so thick they reminded me of toothbrush bristles.

I watched him eat his donut in a fastidious, ladylike way—I noticed that he chose a cake donut, not one with sticky glaze or icing.

When I think of that summer, the two adjectives that come to mind are "hot" and "lonely." Often when I walked through the living room in the morning to get to the kitchen and make coffee, I'd find my mother lying on the couch with a thin afghan over her. "Why are you sleeping here?" I asked her once, and she looked embarrassed and then said something about hot flashes. We were not a family that talked about what my father called "lady things." I'd navigated my period on my own, when I was twelve; my best friend Edie had shown me where the Maxipads were at Walgreens, and a year later, when we wanted to go swimming, how to insert a tampon. When my mother said "hot flashes," I pictured two hands clapping together, like cymbals, and emerging from them, a puff of light.

I'd spent most of my life in this climate, of course, but in my last three years at Northwestern University, and then in Edinburgh, I'd become accustomed to crisper air. I'd become acquainted with the comfort of sweaters and scarves in earthy colors that made me feel beautiful for the first time in my life, like I was no longer the girl I'd been. The transition back to life on the swampy Gulf Coast and in my parents' depressing house the previous two summers hadn't been easy exactly, but those summers I'd spent every waking hour outside of my waitressing jobs with Edie, who made everything else endurable. This summer Edie had an internship caring for spider monkeys, tortoises, and parrots at a wildlife refuge in Ecuador. This was before smartphones and easy access to email. Edie sent me letters once every couple of weeks in her neat cursive, and I sent her letters back in my clunky cursive.

Without Edie, I didn't know what to do with myself after work or on weekends. I spent whole Saturdays in coffee shops reading. Other days I spent at the movies. When the credits began for one movie, I'd quietly slip into another without paying.

When Leonard appeared on that second Donut Friday, I never in a million years would have imagined I'd soon be trading those lonely days in coffee shops and movie theaters for whole days spent in bed with Leonard in his tiny apartment overlooking the ocean. He had over a decade on me. He was, I soon learned, going through a divorce, and had spent much of that "vacation" moving from the house he'd shared with his wife into an apartment not much larger than my dorm room. Also, I had never had the kind of relationship in which post-ejaculation, the guy wasn't immediately itching to get away from me, as though he believed he was now vulnerable to my sorcery.

The thing with Leonard probably wouldn't have happened,

in fact, if it weren't for Shawn, a guy I'd gone to high school with and who was working at the hospital that summer as a mail carrier. Shawn had barely spoken to me in high school, but when he spotted me sitting at that cramped desk with my stack of manuals, he said, "Whoa, Catherine! Is that you? Damn! What have you been up to? What are you doing for lunch?" And I did meet him for lunch, at a little house-turned-café where we ate shrimp po-boys and drank peach iced tea. He said he was getting together with some friends after work. Did I remember Jeffrey and Carlos? They were going to drink tequila on the beach. He said I should come.

I liked the attention at first, being the only girl with three guys, and not just any guys, but guys who'd been cool in high school. Despite how lanky and awkward he was, Shawn had dated chic Jeanette Morrow, whose mother was French.

But soon, I grew uncomfortable. Shawn kept refilling my cup. At some point, he placed his hand on my hip in a firm, confident way, like he'd put his hand on my hip a million times before. He reminded me of my brother, who barged into my room without knocking, and when I said to him, "Can you please knock?" would look at me in his smirking, affronted way. "It's not your room anymore," Rod had said once, and pointed to Mom's sewing machine and the three bolts of fabric atop my old desk. I was afraid of Rod, who was almost four years younger than me but at least fifty pounds heavier, and who had once kicked a hole in the bathroom door because I was taking too long in the shower. Something about the way Shawn touched my hip made me think of Rod and then, glumly, of men in Texas, with their hairy forearms and loud laughs and stupid way of spelling their names, and then, nostalgically, of the men in Scotland, whom months ago I'd found stand-offish and frustratingly difficult to talk to, but now struck me as charmingly shy. I was drunk. My thoughts clunked, like this toddler Kristy I used to babysit for, who never learned to crawl properly, but would drag herself around with her forearms. What was I doing here, on this gritty beach, with these dudes? I felt very sorry for myself.

Anyway, when I removed Shawn's hand from my hip, his face changed, like he'd taken off a mask. He said, "What was that?"

I said, "It's so hot and muggy." Then I said, "I just realized I'm exhausted. And I have work tomorrow. I better head out."

Before I could take a step, though, Shawn caged me in against the back of his Jeep. We were on a secluded part of the beach where you could drive onto the sand if you wanted to. He didn't touch me, but he stretched those long arms out on either side of me, his palms flat against the metal. Suddenly I had the feeling I'd made a terrible mistake. Jeffrey and Carlos were several yards away, talking and laughing. Despite their familiar faces, I didn't really know any of these guys, yet they'd been friends for years. If Shawn decided that my taking him up on his offer to buy lunch and joining him here on the beach and drinking his tequila meant I owed him something, could I count on Jeffery and Carlos to defend me?

Shawn said, "It's just that, damn, you're incredibly sexy. Do you know that?"

Even back then, I got a squirmy feeling when a guy asked if I knew I was pretty or sexy or smart. I couldn't quite have articulated what was so creepy about a compliment being flipped into a question, but I felt manipulated even if I didn't yet have the word for it. Something like that had been going through my head, probably, when I doodled "asking for it" on those sticky notes. Once I learned to recognize the many ways men tried to manipulate women, men rarely tried that with me anymore.

That night, I said, "Seriously, Shawn. I need to get home." I pushed at his arm.

He laughed. "You're going to have to push harder than that."

I surprised myself by saying, "Move or I'm going to kick you in the balls."

His face changed yet again, another mask shed. "You already have," he said.

He stepped away, though, and I walked briskly up the beach toward my car, where I'd left it parked just off the street. I didn't say goodbye to Jeffrey and Carlos, and I could hear them behind me asking Shawn what happened, where was I going.

When I let myself back inside the house, I was close to tears. The drive home had been harrowing—I was drunker than I'd realized—and even though it was nearly midnight and I had work the next morning, what I wanted more than anything was to curl up under the old afghan and watch something stupid on TV. But my mother was already sprawled on the couch, asleep, her mouth open in a way that looked pitiful. The afghan had fallen off her. I looked down at her, at her slightly open mouth and her nightgown riding up on her legs, her thighs doughy, pocked, and almost blue. The nightgown had a tea-colored stain.

I wondered what the hell was going on in my house, if my mother was really suffering from hot flashes or if something deeper was afoot. My parents had never struck me as happy, but now there was something thicker, more solid, about their misery. My mother seemed full of grievances about small, strange things—she'd said to me very bitterly the other day that she'd never in her life gotten to see snow. Sometimes I would catch my parents looking at each other or at my brother in covert ways that I imagined I wasn't intended to intercept, and it made me feel like they were all performing around me, that when I walked out the door they behaved in entirely different ways. It was like a book I had loved when I was a kid: as soon as a child left the room, his toys all came alive and talked to each other.

Was I imagining all this? Or had Edie distracted me in the past from realizing how out of place I was in my own home, how deeply I didn't belong there?

I lay in bed, Shawn's angry, aggrieved face rearing in my mind, and thought about the word "homesick." In my study-abroad materials, there'd been a whole pamphlet about how to cope with homesickness. It had said that homesickness is a feeling of not belonging; we long for home because we tend to associate the feeling of belonging with home. But the word "homesick" seemed a more apt term for what I was feeling—a sickness born of no longer belonging in the place that is, or was, home.

———

In the morning, my brain pushed at my skull, something reptilian, bones and slick green skin, trying to bust out of its too-tight shell. I looked through the medicine cabinet, as well as my mother's not-so-secret stash of meds in her dresser, but all I found were allergy meds, antacid tablets, expired prescriptions for drugs I couldn't pronounce, and my mother's Xanax, which I was pretty certain she was no longer taking. Afraid I'd be late to work if I stopped anywhere, and hence have to endure more than the usual eyebrow raises from Tammy and inappropriate comments from Archie, I guzzled coffee and water and ate two bananas on the drive over.

The sun's glare in the parking lot made me want to claw a hole into the earth to the cool, dark dirt. I dug around my trunk for the umbrella I was pretty sure was in there somewhere—plain black on the outside, neon-colored squiggles on the inside. One of the metal spines bent at a weird angle, making me think of a dog with a limp.

I don't know how long he was watching me, but once I closed the trunk and popped up the umbrella, I turned to find Leonard standing on that gleaming asphalt. He wore dark sunglasses that revealed nothing.

Leonard said, "You have an animal in there?"

"What?"

"In your car," he said, pointing.

I thought he was teasing me, insinuating something lewd. Maybe he was just like the other guys in the office, after all. But then he said, "You were talking. I thought you were talking to a dog or something, but I guess you were just talking to that umbrella?"

I looked up at the umbrella, then back to Leonard. "Shit," I said. "I was mumbling to myself?"

"Not mumbling," Leonard said. "Talking. I heard you crystal clear. 'Where are you hiding from me? I know you're in here.'"

I was too miserable to worry about how crazy I must have seemed. I said, "I have the worst hangover, and I couldn't find any ibuprofen at home."

He smiled. "Come with me. I'll hook you up. I have a colossal stash in my desk drawer."

"Colossal? Should I be worried about *you*?" I said.

"I have sciatica," he said.

I nodded, pretending to know what that was.

When we walked past Tammy's desk I was relieved to see that she wasn't in yet—her bright blue purse wasn't there, one of her garish cardigans wasn't slung over the back of her chair. Leonard led me to his office in the corner. There was a plant on his desk with purple, velvety leaves. "Two? Four?" Leonard asked me, and when I looked at him blankly, he shook out four and handed them to me. I swallowed them.

Leonard removed his sunglasses and I was struck, again, by how beautiful his eyes were—a dark brown that made me think of how Hitchcock had used chocolate syrup in lieu of blood in the famous shower scene in *Psycho*, where the blood pools and then swirls down the drain. I pressed my fingers to my forehead. What was the matter with me? In Evanston and more recently in Scotland I'd felt occasionally lost and lonely, but never like this, like the ground was squishy and I was sinking ankle-deep into it.

"Better?" said Leonard, watching me.

"You mean in a placebo effect kind of way? Because the pills won't kick in for at least twenty minutes, right?"

He smiled. "True. So tell me—what kind of Wednesday night were you having that landed you this headache? Is that usual for you, raging on a work night?"

He wasn't looking at me in that greedy way Archie did. His smile seemed more sympathetic than amused.

"Raging?" I repeated.

His smile faltered. "Wrong word?"

I'd reacted to it because the word had, like an incantation, materialized Shawn's unmasked face—the anger and entitlement that his satisfied confidence had slid away to expose. I felt like I was surrounded by angry men—Shawn, my brother. They were hemming me in and gulping all the air.

Then I registered Leonard's mortified expression and realized I was crying.

"Sorry," I said. "I'm so sorry."

Leonard said, "I'm the one who's sorry." He handed me a box of tissues, asked if I wanted to sit. Then I told this stranger about Shawn, my brother, my mother and her afghan, Edie being in Ecuador. Probably none of what I said was coherent, but Leonard listened. I said, "It's just been a really shitty summer." I apologized again and stood up to go, and that's when Archie said from behind me, "Oh, you got Banana in here. I'll catch you later, Leonard."

I don't know what exactly Leonard saw on my face, but he said coolly to Archie, "Her name's Catherine."

My name in Leonard's mouth, I felt seen. I felt safe.

Shawn wasn't the one to deliver the office mail that day. I wondered if he'd called in sick or traded routes or if there was no routine in the mail room as to who took what route on any given day. I was relieved not to see him.

I spent my lunch break at a plant nursery picking out a new plant for Leonard's desk. When I presented it to him after lunch, I said, "I know you've seen and heard enough from me today, so I'll make this short. This is to say thank you. Also, it's an apology. I was a nut this morning. Anyway, I thought the other one might be lonely all by itself. Oh, it's a succulent, so it doesn't need much water. It's low maintenance."

Leonard looked genuinely touched. "No one's ever given me a plant before."

"Well," I whispered, "No one's ever told Archie to stop calling me 'Banana' before. He's been avoiding me ever since, which has been awesome."

Leonard smiled. Then he said, "Listen, you're not the only one who's been having a horrible summer." That's when he told me about splitting up with his wife, Maria, though at this distance, it's hard to remember which details Leonard told me then and which he filled in later. I recall he spoke quietly, and while he talked, he rotated the succulent in his hands. "My wife and I broke up": I know Leonard said that, because I remember thinking—this was the summer that, like Prince Hamlet, I was immersed in "words, words, words"—that it was interesting he called her a "wife" and not an "ex-wife." Though of course that was also grammatically accurate: their marriage was not technically over. "Wife" may have meant nothing at all.

Leonard's eyes drifted towards his office door. "Catherine,

if you don't mind, please keep all this under your hat. I'm not in the habit of sharing my personal life with co-workers."

"Unlike me, dripping all over you this morning."

"Hey, I'm glad you did. And it feels, weirdly enough, good to talk about this. I've been all—" Leonard mimed a gesture of implosion, like he was a shaken-up bottle of soda. "I've got something I have to do this evening, but maybe we could get a drink after work tomorrow? Something non-alcoholic, I mean," he said, when I winced.

"Peach tea!" I said, so enthusiastically we both laughed. "It's the one thing I like about being home, or more aptly, the-place-that-used-to-be-home: peach tea."

"'The-place-that-used-to-be home,'" Leonard repeated. "Interesting." I think it was that moment my interest in him sparked: not his kindness, or his sticking up for me, or his long-lashed eyes, or even the new information that he was single, but my realization that Leonard was also someone who found language revealing, worth inspection.

—

After work, I stopped by the grocery store to get myself a sandwich from the deli and restock on breakfast items, such as bananas and bagels, I could keep in my bedroom where no one could mistake them as communal property. Nobody cooked dinner that summer. No one did much grocery shopping either. My father worked all the time, so he was rarely home in the evenings. Rod was out a lot, too. When Rod was home, he ate microwave dinners. My parents had a deep freeze in the garage loaded with frozen burgers, corn dogs, mini pizzas, chimichangas, and other junk food. I had no idea what my mother ate or when she ate. I wondered if she went whole days without putting food into her mouth.

In the grocery store, a woman watched me from the other end of the produce section. When I looked up, she looked away. I glanced back at the raspberries, then felt her looking at me again. This happened a few times before I turned toward her so fast that I caught her. I felt like I'd reeled in a tricky fish who'd been nipping at my line. The woman pursed her lips. I realized then that I knew her from somewhere. She was approximately my parents' age, but unlike my mother, this woman put effort into how she looked—misplaced effort, in my opinion (her nails were too long, talon-like, and painted an unflattering coral), but effort nonetheless.

When she wheeled her cart over to me, she said, "You're Rod's sister, right? I'm sorry, I can't remember your name. You were in my middle daughter's class. Stacey King?"

I remembered Stacey. She'd been in the car with another girl, Tamara Scott, when they crashed into a median. Tamara had died. I'd heard that Stacey went into rehab right after graduation.

The woman squinted at me. "Wait, do you not know anything about this?"

"About what?" I said.

"My younger daughter, Sharon, was dating your brother, but she broke up with him a couple months ago. He'd become aggressive with her, which, frankly, doesn't surprise me," she said, bitterness creeping into her voice. "Here's the thing," she continued. "Someone murdered our live oak tree in the middle of the night recently, and I don't think it's a coincidence."

"Murdered?" I said.

"Hacked away at it with an axe. Poisoned it. I've tried calling your parents, but my calls go to voicemail. I don't want to call the police, but I feel like I have no choice."

The grocery store had that bright, hot lighting that all supermarkets do, so when I looked at Stacey King's mother, she seemed spot-lit: not just her strange, boiled-shrimp nails, but the way her lipstick had rubbed off in the corners. There was something a little wild about her eyes. They were so wide open that her pupils were surrounded by white iris, which made them seem like bull's-eye targets. It reminded me of something similarly off-kilter about Stacey King, who I could suddenly picture walking down our high school corridor as if it were the swaying deck of a boat.

It wasn't that Mrs. King, whatever-her-name was, was saying anything implausible. I knew calls in my house went to voicemail. I'd told myself when the phone rang that it wasn't my affair; no one in Galveston was interested in contacting me. And that summer, I would have believed nearly anything about my brother. So I can't really account for the clannishness that kicked in. Nevertheless I said, "Did someone hack your tree, or poison it?"

Mrs. King's eyes opened even wider: her pupils were inner tubes flung into round pools of milk. "What?"

"You're saying my brother 'murdered' your tree, right? So did he poison it or hack it with an ax? Or both? Was the ax's blade poisoned?" I thought of Hamlet again, remembered the poisoned tip of Laertes's sword blade. Would Rod do something so bizarre? Though (or even because) the answer felt obvious, I burst out laughing.

Stacey King's mother shook her head. "You're all crazy," she said, and huffed away, her shoes slapping the tile.

I'd recently seen an Italian horror film, *La Sindrome di Stendhal*, or *The Stendhal Syndrome*, that I couldn't stop thinking about. It was a film about a policewoman who is greatly overcome by a painting, hence the film's title, and soon after that, is attacked by a rapist/murderer. She enters a fugue state, and after knocking her attacker into a river, she becomes possessed by him. She kills her lover, her psychologist, and her police partner, all the while convinced that the guy who attacked her is the one who's murdering the people in her life.

What made the film that much more unforgettable was that the director, Dario Argento, directed his daughter, Asia, in the lead role. It was hardly the first time he'd cast his female family members in his horror films, I'd read. His relationship with Asia's mother, Daria, began on a horror film set years earlier, and the demise of their relationship is said to be traceable in the increasing violence she endures in his films over the years. He'd directed Asia's sister in several films, too, but even years later, when I'd watched many of Argento's other films, *The Stendhal Syndrome* still struck me as one of the most vicious, at least as far as violence toward his female family members goes.

Standing there in that grocery store as Stacey King's mother wrote off my entire family as crazy, I thought about Asia's willingness to allow her father to direct her through her character being raped and tormented on screen. I wondered why she played those roles again and again in his films. I wondered what playing those roles did to her.

I took my sandwich to the seawall, ate it on a concrete bench as seagulls circled above.

Maybe my job was making me paranoid—even if all I did was copyedit manuals, those manuals bristled with information about how one's environment was full of potential menaces. How did one avoid absorbing them? Hospitals, homes. I thought of the hole in our bathroom door. I felt worried, suddenly, for Leonard, putting on his thin blue gloves, and his mysterious role in eradicating whatever it was—spills, things that had seeped where they didn't belong. Like me, I thought, and then smiled at my grandiose vision of myself as some green, glowing puddle, a cartoon version of radioactive waste.

"Hey, I know I made a whole production about peach tea," I said, when we sat down the next evening. "But would you mind if I got a glass of wine instead?"

Leonard raised his eyebrows. "Order whatever you want, Catherine."

Our tabletop was a shiny black wood that reflected a blurry version of my face. Were my eyes really that far apart? I remembered when I was a kid and the princess mask I'd chosen for Halloween was too narrow—the eyeholes hadn't lined up with my eyes. I'd cried, convinced I was a freak, until my mother, in a rare moment of tenderness and maternal command, persuaded me that my own face was a thousand times more beautiful than the princess mask, with its pursed, disapproving lips. Mom had opened a drawer full of lipstick and showed me how to dab the colors on the back of my hand until I chose, finally, a lurid pink.

Sitting with Leonard, I felt a tenderness for my mother that was difficult to reconcile with my other feelings concerning her—disgust, bitterness, disappointment.

I said, "Sometimes I feel like I don't know anyone, and I never will."

Leonard smiled in a sad way. "Me, too."

"Do you think that if everyone felt that way, it would be a little less hard?" I'd received a letter from Edie the previous evening, after returning home from eating my sandwich. She was in love, she'd written, and she would tell me more later. The letter was barely a page. Her previous letters had been so thick, she'd had to tape the envelopes shut. This one had seemed emaciated in comparison. It had made me think of the sad apple mess in a foil pan that my mother made for my birthday one year. When I'd requested apple pie, I'd had Edie's grandmother's pie in mind—bounteous, buttery crust.

"What makes you think they don't?" Leonard said.

Our wine arrived then, and he raised his glass toward mine. We clinked them quietly.

"Because other people seem so satisfied," I said.

Leonard laughed. "They're just better at faking it." But then he became somber and stared, as I had, into the blurry, tabletop reflection of himself. As I got to know Leonard, I became used to these moments—the way he would switch from being present and cheerful to sad, lost in thought. Edie had long told me that I would "go away" like this sometimes. When we were kids, she tried to demonstrate by making her eyes look blank and distant.

To reel Leonard back, I said, "Why do they fake it? So they can feel superior?" I thought of Tammy, how she would narrow her eyes, which flashed through all her make-up like someone peering through a sequined carnival mask.

"I wonder about that. Why pretend to be satisfied? Is it for one's own sake, or to make life easier for other people?" Leonard looked at me intently. "It's a complicated social contract. On the one hand, you don't want to impose your agony on other people. On the other hand, you don't want to shock someone who thinks you're doing fine, who believes you are genuinely contented, by suddenly showing distress—and then blame them for not noticing."

His words have come back to me in recent days, when I encounter those CDC signs in storefronts that say "I wear my mask to protect you; you wear your mask to protect me."

Sitting across from Leonard, I was overcome with a desire to touch his hand. It wasn't simply a matter of that hand belonging to Leonard that made me want to touch it. Something about the bones and even the warm putty color of his skin reminded me of the spindly bodies of Alberto Giacometti's sculptures, which I'd written a paper about for my Art History class the previous fall. His women were always rigid, motionless, their bodies as pointed as arrows, while his men took big strides and shaped the space around them with their long, thin arms.

I'd read that Alberto's wife, Annette, was his sole female model in large part because he was difficult to work with, easily frustrated with models for not sitting still long enough or holding a pose in precisely the way he wanted. I wondered: Did Annette stand as rigidly as he sculpted her? Was that her decision or his? Did she ever long to shape the space around her?

Thinking about Annette was what inspired me finally to

reach across the table and take Leonard's hand. He looked a little surprised, but didn't say anything, didn't remove his hand. I turned it this way and that, as if examining a dug-up artifact.

"I hope this doesn't sound weird, but your hands are strangely beautiful."

"Strangely?" he said.

"They're kind of insect-like."

"That's fine, but since we're being honest, your fingers are disproportionately short," he said.

I was about to tell Leonard that his ears made me think of cup handles when I saw my father walk into the restaurant with a woman who was not my mother.

"It's nothing" was something I kept hearing that summer, and kept telling myself, like some obedient parrot: when I saw my mother sleeping on the couch, her mouth open in that defenseless way; or once saw my brother's knuckles, raw and abraded. You know those cartoons with the angel and the devil perched over someone's shoulders, whispering in each ear? For me, one hovering voice would say "What the fuck?" and the other would counter, immediately, soothingly "It's nothing." Or as Hamlet says, "There is nothing either good or bad, but thinking makes it so."

I straightened so suddenly that Leonard, who had been leaning towards me, smiling, jerked back. The woman with my father was wearing a hot pink cardigan, the kind of cardigan

Tammy might wear, and while I watched, slipped her bright arm through my father's and looked up at him, beaming.

"What the fuck?" I said aloud. I turned to Leonard, who was watching me with alarm—it made me a little abashed how often in the past couple of days I'd seen that expression on his face. "My father," I whispered, and then, "Don't look." Leonard's expression chilled. I said, still whispering, "Not you! That woman. Not my mom."

It was smoke-signal speech, but Leonard, after a moment of looking entirely baffled, said, "Oh."

I slumped in my chair, like I was going to merge, Alice-through-the-looking-glass fashion, into the tabletop reflection of myself.

"Let's get out of here." Leonard flagged the waitress for our check.

———

Since I couldn't very well leave Galveston until school resumed, spending the night at Leonard's apartment a couple times a week was the next best thing. It was cramped, but there was just enough room for two foldout chairs on the balcony overlooking the ocean, so we could both sit and stare sadly out at the water at the same time if we wanted. Early mornings, though, I had the balcony to myself while Leonard slept. I carried a blanket out there to drape over my lap and a brown diner-looking mug of hot coffee. When the tide went out, I'd imagine the ocean was sucking away some of my pain and that when the tide pushed back in, that pain would be diluted.

I saw my father so rarely that summer that it wasn't until a week after spotting him with Pink-cardigan that I saw him again. This was a Sunday morning. He was in the kitchen rolling out dough.

"What are you doing?" I asked despite not wanting to acknowledge him. I was truly bewildered. I'd only ever seen him grill meat or boil pasta. In the weeks I'd been home that summer, nobody had used either the oven or the stove, only that disgusting microwave, the food-splattered inside reminding me of a Pollock painting.

"Making cinnamon rolls." He grinned, slathered the rolled dough in softened butter.

"Want to sprinkle the cinnamon and sugar? You always liked doing that part."

"I don't know what you're talking about."

"What?" He sounded wounded. "We used to make these when you were little."

I looked at him, baffled. There was a trashy book I read over and over when I was a kid, in which the main character, Audrina, is brainwashed by her parents to forget all her traumatic memories. Her parents wipe her mind clear of being molested and raped; they persuade her that she had an older sister who died, whom bad things happened to. I wondered if I was the subject of an opposite kind of brainwashing, where for obscure reasons, my parents had cleared my mind of all happy memories of home, leaving behind only the hole in the bathroom door, Rod going through my mother's purse looking for money for pot, or calling me a controlling bitch. Was I going crazy? Or was I some kind of Replicant with curated, implanted memories, like Sean Young in *Bladerunner*, a perfectly round tear caught, pearl-like, in one of her eyelashes? I stood by my father shaking pinches of sugar and cinnamon on the soon-to-be-coiled dough, wondering if the action ("A little less cinnamon," he said) would retrieve the memory. It didn't.

When I told Leonard about the cinnamon rolls and my various theories while we lay in his bed one evening, he said, "Or maybe we all move in and out of parallel universes without realizing it. Maybe your dad did make cinnamon rolls with you when you were a kid, but with a different version of you, not *you* you." He pressed two fingers to the hard plate of my sternum.

"And in that other universe, he's married to the woman in the pink cardigan, so he doesn't realize that in this universe, he's cheating?"

Leonard winced. "Yeah, bad theory. But it is stunning sometimes just how different people's versions of things are."

I would think about Leonard's words later that October after my father told me in a brief letter folded up inside a card printed with Mary Cassatt's painting *Young Woman Reading* that he was leaving my mother. And again, when a few days later I received the exact same card from my mother (almost certainly the stationery was hers and rather than buy a card of his own, my father had taken one of my mother's cards), hers explaining that they were taking "a little breather" from each other, as if marriage were akin to swimming underwater.

—

After that summer, I didn't return home for over six years.

I use the word "home" to mean the place to which I am native, the place where I came into being, as opposed to the place where I belong. Every time I think of "home," I think of that day in Leonard's office, when he repeated me. When he said "'The-place-that-used-to-be-home.' Interesting," and looked at me as if *I* was interesting; I was a puzzle he was trying to figure out.

And I remember the sudden blue flame of interest that ignited in me. I looked into Leonard's brown eyes and felt like here, in this alien place where I was from and yet out of place, there was a kindred spirit ("kindred spirit" was what my father called Paulette, when he finally told me about her). Leonard was another person who cared about words.

Only it turned out he didn't really care about words in the way I do. What made me and Leonard split up before I went back to Northwestern (as opposed to after, which would have inevitably happened) was a conflict about language.

One of the few things he had told me about Maria, his "wife" (I'm using Leonard's language here. I never heard him call Maria his ex) was that things had soured between them when they "lost" their baby. "It was like she went into her corner, I went into mine," he said, and then looked down and away, like he had indeed retreated into some low mouse hole in the wall. I squeezed his hand to convey I was listening, but the subject was clearly closed.

It wasn't until nearly the middle of August, when we were at his friends Fred and Rena's. Rena was grilling sausages, and I remember thinking that was cool and non-gender normative, that the wife was grilling sausages. I liked Rena, with her salamander tattoo on her shoulder and her authoritative way of holding tongs, turning the sausages carefully so they blistered on the grill. I was trying to make a good impression, which meant I was only half-listening to Rena, because I was busy composing witty or thoughtful sentences in my head. So when she said "miscarriage" I didn't immediately get what she was saying, and Rena said it again, smiling at me: "This is the happiest I've seen Leonard, since Maria had the miscarriage."

Hearing Rena say that word "miscarriage" twice, Leonard's word, "lost," bothered me in a new way. I remembered hearing the word "vagina" for the first time at Jenny Butler's sleepover when I was in about the fourth grade. My mother had always referred to that region of the body as "lady bits."

What Leonard had done was different, but on another level, it was the same: he'd deliberately withheld information from me, and now here I was in Fred's and Rena's backyard realizing I was the only person there who didn't already know that Maria had had a miscarriage in the first trimester of pregnancy (as opposed to the baby dying at birth or after, which is what I'd imagined given the very limited information Leonard supplied).

Suddenly, Leonard seemed like my parents—shrouding and avoiding what makes him uncomfortable, not thinking about how those choices affect the people he purports to care about.

I had trouble articulating why I felt so betrayed, though, even to myself: I tried writing Leonard a note and got fixated on the word "misled"—it looked bizarre to me, unreal, like a word I would have made him look up in the *Scrabble* dictionary. So I never explained to Leonard why I was upset. I just made excuses, and he looked at me with sad, puzzled eyes. My last day at work, he said, "Well, goodbye, Catherine."

When I returned to Galveston six years later, it was for Edie. Her stepfather had died suddenly of a heart attack, right after Thanksgiving, and she didn't want to be alone with her family, either. So she flew from Seattle to Albuquerque, and we drove to Texas together, shared a hotel room on the beach. We accomplished every item on the to-do list together: I sat next to Edie on the pew in my only black dress, squeezing her hand; she accompanied me to the house my father shared with Paulette and

which Paulette had decorated for Christmas by putting up a
fake tree in every room of the house, the tree in the kitchen the
same pink as that cardigan from years earlier ("It's like we're in
that Dr. Seuss book with all the colorful trees," Edie whispered);
I accompanied Edie to dinner at a crab place with her dad and
his uber-Christian girlfriend, Linda, who, judging by her weird
questions about why I was there and the way she hardly met my
eyes, probably thought Edie and I were lovers; she accompanied
me to the house I'd grown up in, where my mother still lived, and
where she still lay on the couch with an afghan over her lap, as if
no time had passed.

On our last night we got margaritas at the bar Leonard had
first taken me to, the bar we'd scuttled out when my Dad walked
in with Paulette. I only remembered it was the same place when I
looked down at my drink and encountered my wobbly reflection,
as if it had been waiting for me these six years.

"Where's Catherine?" said Edie in that singsong way she'd
been doing that since we were ten.

"This was where," I began to say. Then I stopped, remembering that I'd never told Edie much about Leonard, except, in an
early letter, that I'd bought this kind guy at work a plant. But
I hadn't told her about sleeping with him, about those nights I
sheltered in his tiny apartment and wrapped myself up in a gray
blanket, drinking my coffee and watching the lulling, back-and-
forth motion of the waves tongue the beach. Why hadn't I told

her? I supposed because Edie had been in love then, so smitten with Miguel—her letters had seemed all the more full of Miguel because they were so short, like small weights that are surprisingly heavy. And it seemed wrong to respond to those letters by telling her about Leonard, weird and pathetic, like I was trying, once again, to close the gap between cheerful, well-loved Edie, with her grandmother-baked, fat, oozy apple pies, and my own desiccated life.

So, though Edie was looking at me expectantly, I just shook my head. There was no point in telling Edie about Leonard now. He'd been like a Band-Aid that summer—a useful but flimsy Band-Aid that had soon enough gone gray at the edges and fallen off.

Instead, I reached across the table and took Edie's hand as I had once taken Leonard's. I realized homesickness for me had never been a longing for a particular place, but for this particular person.

FAMILY REUNION: INVENTORIES

Number of times her Uncle Stetson said she should visit the family more often: IIII.

Words on the shampoo bottles crowded into the shower rack in the bathroom she had to share with her cousin Kayla and Kayla's husband and kids: Pert, Suave, Swagger.

Words she located inside those words: use, rage, wager, sweat, pervert, trap.

Times she cut her leg shaving because her Aunt Birdie rapped on the door and said, "Make sure you don't use up all the hot water, Hon": II.

Items hatch marks reminded her of: prison bars, cypresses, the teeth of a steel comb.

Sticky things encountered: buttercream frosting smeared inside a piping bag; a stain on the bedcover she doesn't want to contemplate; Kayla's husband Harrison's eyes that move down her body like suction cups, leaving a tarry trail where they adhere.

Number of dead flies in the kitchen sink basin at one time: IIII.

What was most beautiful about dead flies, when examined closely: not (as one would imagine) their faceted eyeballs, rather their fuzzy, plier-like feet.

Lies she considered before eventually telling her dad (her "poor dad whose kids never visit" according to Uncle Stetson) that, yes, she could make the family reunion this year, after all: she broke a femur and can't hardly get out of bed; she's developed a phobia of flying; she volunteers at a soup kitchen and they're short-staffed.

Things that make her tired: playing Go Fish with Kayla's daughters Sandy and Alexis, Sandy crying every time she has to give up her queens, Kayla saying to Sandy, "Paige used to cry every time she lost at checkers."

Things she has in common with these people: DNA, except in the case of in-laws, such as Harrison, who most definitely did not answer when she knocked on the bathroom door that afternoon and asked if anyone was in there; towels, like the pale blue one she'd used to dry her hair, spotted wrapped around Harrison's waist when she opened the door.

Instances in which her dad embarrassed her, while simultaneously breaking her heart: when his eyes glistened at Kayla's announcement that she is pregnant again (actually she said, "we," gesturing to Harrison, as though he would be carrying her uterus around part-time like a Baby Bjorn); when he whispered during a viewing of *Terms of Endearment* that he wished she had a better relationship with her sister; when he said between bites of lasagna that the more educated your children are, the farther away from home they move.

Number of people at the table insulted by her dad's pronouncement: III, maybe more.

Retaliation in response to her dad's pronouncement: her Uncle Stetson saying, "Communication studies? What will they come up with next? Handshake studies? Coffee thermos studies?"; Kayla's loud laugh in response.

Scavengers sighted from the house's screened-in porch: raccoons, yellowjackets, black vultures, turkey vultures.

Nicknames for her: "Bangs," due to the allegedly loud way she opened cabinets, looking for the coffee beans. In conflict with that one, "Mumbles," because when Aunt Birdie asked her if she has a boyfriend, she saw Harrison across the room listening, his whole body straining to listen. He was a six-foot crenellated ear, drinking a beer.

Things that could happen to her if she doesn't sit up straight: spinal curvature, no job offers because interviewers like confident young women, never being asked to dance because of being without grace.

Wildflowers growing on the property: bluebonnets, Indian paintbrushes, Indian blankets, winecups, fleabane, Texas thistle, spiderwort, prickly pear cactus blossoms, sunflowers, Blackfoot daisies.

What, four days later, she realized she has in common with Aunt Birdie, after all: they both love the word "potpourri." "You too?" they said, upon discovering this. All day long, Kayla looking at them like they were juvenile and Harrison like he was wondering why he ever bothered staring at her tits, she and Aunt Birdie cracked each other up intoning "Potpourri, potpourri, potpourri."

DISAGREE TO DISAGREE

 Charlie in what she has come to think of as teenagers' natural habitat: standing in front of the open refrigerator door, looking aggrieved. "Good morning," Anne says, forcing cheer into her voice.

"I'm starving," says Charlie.

Anne reaches past her for the coffee, and begins spooning it into the filter, maintaining, as she does, a kind of internal commercial jingle: I will not engage, I will not engage. She could mention all the options from yesterday's grocery shop—the bag of nectarines, the very expensive cherries from Spain, yellow and pink, that she bought because Charlie loves cherries, the cabinet full of cereal, the Eggo waffles and breakfast sausages in the freezer—but Charlie has eyes; Charlie can see all these items perfectly well herself. She could remind herself what Charlie's advisor said: that teenagers use complaint as a means of preserving intimacy, to communicate to their parents, in the flat-footed way adolescents do, that they are still needed, that their children still depend upon them. She could also snap, which is the most tempting thing to do, really the default response. But in the tally board in her head that has her household on the left side and Ethan's on the right, this would be one more demerit, one more piece of evidence that Ethan's house is the desired location, and hers, not so much. Hers is the Casa of Suck. Ethan's wife probably makes Charlie French toast with homemade Challah bread.

Anne remembers something she read in the textbook for the anthropology course she took in the fall—how humans have the longest period of infant dependency of any primate. And how this prolonged dependence has long been a burden to mothers in particular, limiting the kinds of work they can do outside of childcare. Duh, she'd thought. That was why in her mid-thirties she was taking night classes, incrementally earning her B.A. Because despite what she'd said when she got pregnant with Charlie about how she was going to finish her degree and work, not become one of those obsessive mothers who get fidgety even when their own family members hold the baby, she had dropped out. All those years ago when Anne showed the smug woman at the daycare, Barb was her name, the breast milk she'd packed in the insulated tote bag, Barb had said, "Looks like you packed enough milk for everyone in the infant room." That word, *everyone*, had clung to Anne like a burr. She couldn't stop picturing Barb sucking on one of the rubber nipples. How could she leave Charlie with that woman after that?

Also this: Ethan had urged Anne to stay home with Charlie. But years later, he insisted he had merely indulged her. He said Anne had clearly wanted to be home with Charlie, so he'd assured her that if she wanted to, she could and she should.

The anthropology textbook offered hunting as an example of work that was incompatible with child care. Next to that chunk of text was a photograph of a woman tending a garden, a sleeping infant strapped onto her back. Anne raised her hand in class and said, "Prolonged infant dependency? My kid's fourteen, and she acts like frying an egg is as taxing as hunting a wildebeest."

The professor said, "There's a theory that human children grow and mature slowly as a kind of survival mechanism. Remaining small and immature elicits caretaking from adults. It also makes children less threatening." She then talked about how in orangutan populations in which life is particularly stressful or competitive, the young will remain physically and behaviorally immature into adulthood. It's like somehow their bodies know it's not safe yet to grow.

"I'm starving!" Charlie says, again. Sometimes Charlie will go a good half hour repeating a single phrase: "Where is my phone?" for example. It reminds Anne of that scene in *The Wire*, where two of the police detectives, McNulty and Moreland, for five minutes utter nothing but the word "Fuck." One of them picks up a discarded gun, says "Fuck." Another looks out a window: "Fuck." To Ethan, this scene was evidence that *The Wire* was overrated. "How could that show be nominated for writing awards?" But to Anne, it was brilliant, an example of how much communication could occur extra-verbally.

What if "I'm starving" is the only phrase Charlie will utter, ever again? What if she is permanently language impaired, like that nymph Echo in Greek mythology, cursed so she can only repeat, or like Ethan's stroke-struck mother, who can only remember names of certain tropical fruits?

Anne hears the professor's words again: Survival mechanism. She thinks of one of the tips she'd read in an article about how to help children cope with divorce: Help your child put her feelings into words. Would Anne eventually, with practice, be able to distinguish the meaning behind the phrase, to discern when "I'm starving" meant "I love you," when it meant "Fuck you"?

"Let's go out for breakfast then," Anne says. "Let's go to that place that puts out the cookies and coffee while you wait to get seated."

They'd gone there a couple times when it was still the three of them, but both times Ethan found fault with his order. The first time his eggs were over easy rather than over medium. The second time his tomatoes didn't taste like tomatoes. "These are the sad tomatoes," he said. Sad tomatoes: that's what he called commercial tomatoes, the kind you find at fast food restaurants and some of the less pricey grocery stores. For a man who neither cooked nor gardened, Ethan had strong opinions about food. Tomatoes should, for instance, smell like sweet dirt.

Charlie says, "I love those cookies!" and Anne feels a strange satisfaction, as though her suggestion is as good as baking the cookies herself.

The café is only about a mile and a half away and the morning cool, so they walk. Charlie is wearing cut-offs that give new meaning to the word "short." Anne hates this look, where you can see the white inside pockets dangling below the frayed cuffs. Those pockets make her think of "I surrender" handkerchiefs. It's as though by exposing them, Charlie is announcing that her body is available for the taking. Of course, this is terribly un-feminist, so Anne refrains from saying it. But it makes Anne want to weep, the way these girls dress. She wonders what her anthropology professor would have to say about their black eyeliner and skimpy crop tops and denim diapers. How would Professor Feingold reconcile this mode of attire with her theory about the protracted childhood of orangutans? Every time a car drives by, Anne is on high alert. She expects to see leaning out a window some hairy, low-browed man, with a gorilla's hole-punch nostrils.

"I don't get why exposed umbilical cord scars are supposed to be sexy anyway," Anne says.

"Gross," Charlie says.

"That's precisely what it is. Proof that you were once tethered to my uterus."

Charlie makes a face. But Anne's words have their desired effect; Charlie pulls at the bottom of her shirt.

Then Charlie says, "I've seen those photos of you in that rainbow-colored tube top. And Dad has that shaggy hair."

Absurdly, Anne feels sad that she got rid of that tube top, though she wouldn't dream of wearing it now, even if she could pull it off, which she most certainly cannot.

"I never said I'm not a hypocrite," Anne says.

An elderly man is approaching in the opposite direction. He shows no sign of moving out of the way, which means if neither person moves, they're going to collide. In fact, he's looking at the houses on the opposite side of the road, not the least bit mindful about what's in front of him. Anne is suddenly seething. Always it's men who enact these games of chicken.

When they're a few yards apart, and Charlie is yanking on Anne's arm, Anne stops in her tracks and waits for the man to notice her. When he finally does, he stops and says, "Excuse me."

"You're on the wrong side of the sidewalk," Anne says.

"What?" he says.

Charlie looks as stunned as he does. Anne remembers the time she came home with a cake that read "You Said You Hate Me" in purple icing. Anne can't remember now what Charlie was angry about that day, only that she'd felt a weird mix of happy and sad when Charlie said those words. Happy because Charlie was more startled than she was, immediately apologized. Sad that it hadn't occurred to her to appreciate that Charlie had never said anything like that to her before. Since it was too late to buy Charlie a cake for not saying she hated her mother, Anne settled for a cake to celebrate that she had said it.

"Mom," says Charlie, tugging her arm. What if Charlie were limited forevermore to the word "Mom"? What does this particular "Mom" mean? It doesn't sound, to Anne's ear, like the mortified iteration she is most familiar with, "Mo—om!," drawn out to express how lengthily and deeply Anne humiliates her daughter. No, it sounds more like Charlie is frightened. But why frightened? Anne studies the man in front of her. This guy is old. He must be at least eighty. Surely Anne could take him in a fight.

Anne looks him in the eye; he looks back at her, folding his arms.

She thinks of a Dr. Seuss book she used to read Charlie, the one about the North-going Zax whose path is obstructed by a South-going Zax. Neither of them give way. Both fold their furry, Seuss-creature arms, exactly like this dude. Slowly, the city gets built around them; they are a truculent island, girdled in overpasses. As a kid, Charlie was mystified by the two Zaxes. "Why won't they just move?" she asked Anne, and Anne said, "Because sometimes—" and then faltered, unable to complete the thought.

The most dangerous primates, Professor Feingold told them, are the old ones, because they have the most to prove. Challenged by a much bigger young male, one aging orangutan clubbed him on the head with a tree branch and killed him. In general, the dangerous animals aren't the ones you'd expect, a fellow student pointed out. In Yellowstone, the animals that caused the most fatalities were not bears but deer, cornered by tourists wanting to take their pictures.

—

"You're the one who always tells me not to go looking for trouble," Charlie says.

"I wasn't looking. I just kind of stumbled onto it."

"He looked so mad! If he were in a cartoon, smoke would have come out of his ears."

"Really?" Anne says, surprised. To her, the old man looked not angry so much as bewildered. He reminded her of her former mother-in-law, who long before the stroke that reduced her vocabulary to "mango," "papaya," and "coconut," had pronounced life too confusing to follow. "I've learned all my brain can learn," Lois told Anne, who was trying to teach her how to use the laptop she and Ethan had bought her for Christmas. "I can't learn anything else." Later, Anne pictured the blood clot that caused Lois's stroke as a globule of data her brain refused to assimilate.

Anne takes a third bite-size cookie from the white tray, and Charlie says, "That reminds me. I signed us up for the band bake sale."

"Us?" Anne says.

"Cookies, brownies, cupcakes—doesn't matter what, as long as I bring two dozen individual bags tomorrow morning."

"What are you going to bake?" Anne says.

Charlie says, "I was thinking you'd make those bars with the chocolate and cranberries."

"I thought your dad was picking you up at four today," Anne says.

"Yeah?" Charlie says. "I mean I guess I could ask Kay to help me if that's what you want. She does love to bake."

At the mere mention or thought of Kay's name, Anne smells ginger. The reverse is true too: if she smells or tastes ginger, Kay's smiling face sprouts from the spicy ginger like the pesky follicle of dark hair that keeps returning on her abdomen no matter how many times she plucks it.

The first time she met Kay was at a ginger beer stand at the farmer's market. By the time she saw Ethan, it was too late to pretend she hadn't seen him. He smiled and waved, hurried over to hug Anne and introduce her to Kay. And that was how Anne's favorite drink, ginger beer, had been ruined.

When she told her best friend, Tia, about the ginger-Kay connection, Tia said, "Nasal hallucinations. That's a sign of disease, you know."

"I'll gladly *help* you," Anne says to Charlie. "But you can't go sign up for a bake sale and then pawn the baking off onto someone else."

Charlie gives her one withering stare, turning the space between them black and crackly, carbonized, and then averts her face in disgust. "You always make such a big deal out of everything," she mutters.

Anne knows, having heard this assessment before, that this is the most damning of insults, though she doesn't really get it. She concedes that the "You Said You Hate Me" cake was making a big deal, and mixing mocktails with sparkling cider and maraschino cherries when Charlie got her first period was making a big deal. But how was saying "So who is this Aaron?" last week, in the lightest and most casual of ways, making a big deal? And wouldn't making a big deal out of the bake sale involve hopping up and down, clapping her hands, and tying matching mom-and-daughter aprons around their waists?

"All I'm saying," Anne begins, then pauses. She suspects that she is about to fall on her knees, crying: please let me bake all your chocolate cranberry bars! Charlie is like a bad boyfriend she keeps begging to forgive her.

"Whatever," Charlie says, and Anne decides that "Whatever," rather than "I'm starving" or "Mom," is really the perfect expression for a one-word Charlie. "Whatever" has range. It can connote peaceful flexibility: "What do you want for dinner?" "Whatever!"

It can be singsong and buoyant. Or it can be scathing as hell.

"Never mind. I'll bake with Kay," Charlie says.

Forget about following your instinct, Dr. Baum, the therapist Anne had seen after splitting with Ethan, used to tell her. Instinct was lizard-brain reaction, and often misguided. Think instead about what you actually want, he said.

Does Anne want to spend her afternoon shopping for cranberries (where will she find cranberries in June)? Does she want to melt chocolate in a double boiler? No, Anne decides, she does not.

"Great idea," Anne says, and Charlie takes a startled bite of her cookie.

For Ethan's house, Kay planted a garden to attract hummingbirds. While Anne wrestles, unsuccessfully, with making concoctions for the hummingbird feeder, the hummingbirds zippily flock to Kay; Kay is a Disney princess with birds perched on her shoulder. Kay tried to explain to Anne once what bright, velvety flowers and vines to plant—which ones attract honeybees and birds—but Anne was like Lois refusing to assimilate new information. No, no, no was what her brain had to say, when Kay tried to spoon into it these bird-enticing plants.

Charlie doesn't speak a word throughout breakfast except to the waitress when she orders crêpes with strawberries and whipped cream. From their table at the edge of the restaurant's patio, she stares out at the street.

Anne used to pride herself on how coolly she handled Charlie's silences. Ethan, on the other hand, would demand that Charlie talk to him, particularly during meals. Refusal to engage in conversation over food was a deadly sin in Ethan's book. "Talk or else ______," he used to say, filling the blank with all manner of threats, from no visiting her grandparents for spring break to no more private trombone lessons. Charlie would go on eating and staring out the window as though she couldn't see or hear Ethan at all. Usually Anne quietly observed Ethan when he let Charlie get the better of him. Then later in their bedroom, when Charlie wasn't around to hear, she'd remind him once again that he was never going to win the battle unless he drastically changed his strategy.

But one time Ethan got so angry that he reached over and took Charlie's plate from her, put it between his and Anne's plates. They were eating tacos, Anne remembers. Charlie's favorite food. Tacos Anne prepared with lettuce and yellow cherry tomatoes she'd picked up at the farmer's market that morning. Tacos Anne made because Charlie was suffering cramps and she'd wanted to do something nice for her. Charlie didn't react. She wiped guacamole from her lip, rested her hands in her lap. But when Ethan took Charlie's plate, Anne lost it. She'd not only returned the plate to Charlie, she'd screamed at Ethan that he had no right to wield the dinner she'd made as a bargaining chip or punishment.

Charlie didn't eat the tacos. She sat there at the end of the table, looking back and forth between Anne and Ethan. Anne, refusing to look at Ethan, gazed back at Charlie. Was Charlie waiting to see if one of them would back off? Bracing herself for what would happen if neither of them did? "Why won't either of them move?" Anne remembered Charlie asking, bewildered, about that North-going and South-going Zax, locked in their face off, as the city loops, a slinky, around them.

Anne watches her daughter stare at pedestrians, studies her profile, her lovely, mollusk-like ear. Charlie is stubborn as hell. Well, she gets it on both sides, a double dose, like the recessive genes that gave her blue-green eyes.

What does Anne find so moving about Dr. Seuss's Zaxes? She wonders, stirring the granola in her yogurt into a whorl. They do not strike her as pure antagonists. They are not opposites, after all. They are alike. And by both refusing to move, they maintain a relationship.

A week after the taco fiasco, Ethan moved out.

Anne and Ethan were oddly matched in so many ways. Anne often summed up their dynamic as "agree to disagree." About having more children, for instance—Ethan had been so freaked out when she got pregnant at twenty-one, but then his philosophy morphed into, if you have one, you may as well have four. He wanted kids two years apart, so they'd be close. Easy for him to campaign for more kids, when the parenting mostly fell to Anne. Anne teased him that it was all an excuse to buy bunkbeds.

When he talked about how lonely he had been, as an only child, she said, merrily, "Let's agree to disagree."

"I disagree to disagree!" That was almost his parting line. The box he'd checked, filing for divorce, was "Irreconcilable differences."

Charlie had remained quiet throughout most of it, even when Anne and Ethan had sat down with her to explain their joint custody arrangement.

When the waitress drops off the check, she smiles sympathetically at Anne. She's young, a college student perhaps. When Anne was her age, Charlie had been a newborn; Anne had worn her everywhere in a sling. Charlie had liked to suck on Anne's finger for so long that her fingertip turned pruney. Ethan called the baby, "your barnacle."

The waitress must observe so much bad behavior in her line of work: an anthropologist, studying the primates.

Anne has long been ambivalent about dining out of the house with Ethan and Charlie for this reason. On the one hand, the break from cooking is welcome. On the other hand, to dine in a restaurant is to put your relationships on display. Of course, it's only when there's tension that Anne feels exposed. She thinks of *Clash of the Titans,* which she watched a dozen times as a kid. Zeus moves about stone figurines representing the human characters like they're dolls in a dollhouse, puts them face-to-face with monsters. Then he watches to see what they'll do. When

faced with some challenge from Charlie or Ethan in a public setting, Anne feels like one of those stone figurines. That everyone
is watching and whatever move she makes will be discussed, ana-
lyzed. Maybe this is part of why she can't stop thinking about the
Zaxes. The way their paths run into each other like that, it's not
an accident. Seuss is their Zeus, forcing them into a test they are
predestined to fail.

SUN SPOTS

THIS MORNING, I EUTHANIZED THE CAT I adopted a week before I met my husband. The cat was twenty, which means my relationship with Jeff is twenty years old, too. The difference is my marriage isn't dead, not yet. But that doesn't mean I haven't thought about killing it. I thought about euthanizing my cat for three years before I made the appointment. Three years Caspian's been on medication. Three years he's been so blind and deaf that he couldn't find his food unless I led him to it. Then seven months ago he started urinating outside his litter box, and I realized how good I'd had it, after all. Seven months is a long time to tolerate the smell of cat piss in your laundry room, to clean up puddles of it with gloved hands and Clorox wipes. When the kids said they couldn't believe I was going to kill the cat, I told them I was doing right by the cat, the cat was in pain. But the real reason was because I was tired of cleaning up cat piss.

My friend Martha and I call our vet "Dr. Hollywood" because he's ridiculously handsome, in an old studio way—long-lashes, a cleft chin. "It will soothe him if you pet him," he told me, so I stroked Caspian, crouched on a fuzzy green blanket on my lap. I'd avoided petting Caspian for weeks. He couldn't clean himself anymore, so his fur was greasy, and he was so bony, poor guy, that I could feel the knobs of his vertebrae, the flared bellows of his ribs. Caspian felt more like something architectural than a living creature, like one of the model planes Jeff begins building and then abandons. Also, he had these nasty little spots, *lesions* Dr. Hollywood called them, on his ears from all the time he spent sitting on windowsills. Solar dermatitis. The first time Dr. Hollywood biopsied to check for squamous cell carcinoma, he recommended I rub sunscreen into Caspian's nearly hairless, pink ears whenever he sat in a window. I did that twice maybe. Then I stopped.

The euthanasia took place on a patch of fake grass that I'd only ever seen through the windows of Dr. Hollywood's exam rooms. There's a hummingbird feeder out there and a real tree, lilac. Now in late May, it still has a few blooms left—heavy masses that make me think of clumps of grapes.

Dr. Hollywood sedated Caspian before bringing him to me—"so she doesn't try to bolt over the wall," he said, and I laughed because 1) Caspian can't even leap up onto our sofa anymore and 2) despite having taken Caspian to Dr. Hollywood for eight years now, he and every technician in that clinic still refer to Caspian as "she." Jeff says it's the name I chose—it's feminine. "What about it is feminine?" I've asked, but Jeff never offers anything concrete to support his point. He says that just because he can't explain it doesn't make it untrue. "It's like how you talk about photography," he says. "You just have a feeling. You just know."

On the patch of fake grass is a wrought iron bench painted a cheerful orange. This is where I sat holding Caspian on the fuzzy green blanket, which encased a pee pad. Dr. Hollywood warned me that it's not uncommon for animals to urinate or defecate as the pentobarbital enters their system.

Caspian looked up at me with his light blue eyes: the prettiest thing about him, the feature that made me pick him out of the litter twenty years ago. They complimented his grey fur, like gas jets flaring through smoke. Dr. Hollywood loomed over me. He's one of those formal vets who wears a white coat and tie, unlike my dentist Timothy, who gossips about his husband and sends me texts asking for my Moroccan spice rub recipe.

I felt like Dr. Hollywood was judging me. I knew it was stupid to feel that way—how many hundreds of animals had he put to sleep, after all? But maybe they'd actually been in pain, as opposed to merely old, greasy, and incontinent.

Caspian's eyes looked accusing, but perhaps light blue eyes always do.

Our daughter Bridget gave me the hardest time about killing Caspian—"killing," she said last night, with a snap, when I had said "putting him to sleep." Bridget is fourteen. Lately, conversation with her feels like a complicated sword fight, both of us doing back flips and swinging on branches to achieve higher ground. "He's in pain!" I said, and Bridget glared at me and said "He's just old!" Then she launched into a whole treatise from that animal rights ethicist, Peter Singer. Animals weren't there for our use, Bridget scolded, every word a flashing blade; animals didn't exist to sustain and entertain us. In response, I looked pointedly at her leather Doc Martens. "Mini-me," my friend Martha used to call Bridget, because she was such a Mama's girl, wanting to do whatever I did: knit, hike, take pictures. These days I'm the one inadvertently mimicking her, except it's the chilly sneer, the eyebrows incredulously raised.

Bridget wasn't out of bed yet this morning when I shoved Caspian into his carrier—even at under six pounds, he doesn't go into that box easily—and I was grateful. In fact, nobody was up when I left the house with Caspian, not that I left particularly early. A quarter til nine. The sun had been up for three hours, as had I. My nine-year-old, Parker, may have been awake reading in bed. He'll stay in bed reading until past lunch on weekends if we don't force him to come out and eat something. Jeff, well, he's practically nocturnal these days. What's weird is that for years, it was the opposite. I was the night owl. Jeff was the one who was fussy about his bedtime. When did that change?

After making coffee, I gave Caspian a special meal— chunks of salmon that had been preserved in a vacuum-sealed pouch. Expensive food I only bought for him a couple times a year because, like my friend Martha says, cat food shouldn't cost more than human food (though I imagine Bridget would have something to say about that assertion). After I held the bowl close to Caspian's face, he inhaled it just as he inhales the gloppy canned paté I usually give him. I wondered if he tasted the difference in price.

Then I sat out on the porch taking measure of everything else dead or dying—the crunchy, pale brown snap pea vines; the leggy squash plants; the flimsy stalks of corn; the bolted parsley. It reminded me of a dystopian film: the city scape in *Bladerunner*, the buildings all abandoned and burnt, blown-out husks. For the first time in years, I longed for a cigarette.

Yesterday, I'd winced when the new hygienist Elaine was cleaning my teeth. My favorite hygienist, Mary Beth, had left the prior year when she had a baby. Jeff claimed Elaine was in fact a better hygienist—she got his teeth cleaner, he said, and I couldn't dispute it—but cleanings had never hurt with Mary Beth, and she was much friendlier. She always asked me about my kids. She remembered not just their names but their personality traits, like the fact that Parker loved graphic novels. While Elaine aimed the water pic, I lay there missing Mary Beth, thinking of the things I would have updated her on about the kids: that Bridget now identified as a Marxist, for instance. "How's Jeff?" she would have asked, and I would have rolled my eyes, making her laugh.

When my dentist came to check on me after Elaine had finished up, I pointed towards the corner of my mouth that had hurt, and Timothy nodded and said there was root exposure. He told me different things he could do, if it started bugging me at home: seal the exposed root. He pointed to the X-ray on the screen. My left molar had bone loss. "If it gets too bad, we can pull that tooth to protect the one next to it," he said. "Better to lose one tooth than to have it infect its neighbor."

It was the same logic I'd applied to my garden when I uprooted the aphid-ridden kale a month ago, so that the aphids wouldn't spread, not that I was confident the aphids wouldn't manage to spread to anything else they wanted anyhow. After all, they'd appeared on the kale out of nowhere.

Caspian is the third cat I've had since I graduated college decades ago, but he's the first I've euthanized. The first cat, Paul Bunyan, was hit by a car. The second, Sim, just disappeared. I like to imagine some lonely old lady adopted him, someone who would comb his fur with a special brush.

Jeff said last night, "No more cats after Caspian."

"What? No way," I said.

"You haven't enjoyed that cat for years. All you've done is complain about him," Jeff said, while he aggressively scrubbed our cast iron pan like he was punishing it.

I said nothing. I studied the splotch of red on and around the pimple on the back of his neck where he'd asked me to help him rub sunscreen in the other day. The range of motion in his right shoulder has been lacking since he tweaked it in the gym. I had been in the middle of photographing a hawk resting on a limb of a palo verde when Jeff came outside and asked for my help, his voice so loud that the hawk immediately took off. "You're always ruining my shots," I'd said. Jeff had flinched. "Sorry for bothering you." He quietly closed the sliding door.

Before Dr. Hollywood connected the syringe with the pentobarbital to the IV protruding from Caspian's right front ankle, which was wrapped in pink surgical tape, he first administered an anesthetic to put Caspian to sleep. Within seconds, Caspian's body went limp and folded in on itself like a children's jumping castle being deflated. Only his eyes were still open. They weren't focused on anything. Dr. Hollywood said, "I forgot to warn you about that. They stay open." Then he held up the second syringe and said, "Ready?" I wondered if anyone ever changed their mind at this point. What would Dr. Hollywood say if they did?

I nodded and kept petting Caspian even though I knew he couldn't feel anything. I kept petting him even after Dr. Hollywood checked his heart with his stethoscope and confirmed that it had stopped beating.

What I thought about as I stroked my dead cat's thin, bumpy ears was Jeff's sunburned neck. After a few minutes of sulking the other morning once Jeff scared off the hawk, I'd gone inside and taken the sunscreen from him, squeezed it onto my fingertips. "I just wish you'd pay closer attention," I'd said.

He'd kept his lips clamped shut, as if he were afraid if he opened them an inadvertent apology might slip out. Or perhaps something else he was afraid to say?

When I'd rubbed the sunscreen in, I'd cringed at the pimple smack dab in the middle of his neck. I didn't want to touch it. As I watched him brutally scrub the pan last night, the sunburn looked round and almost inviting, like a button I might decide to press.

NIGHT VISION

THEY WERE COOLING OFF IN AMANDA'S pool—three women submerged to their necks. With the moon behind them and the stringed lights on Amanda's porch ungenerous in their glow, Amanda's and Louise's faces were silhouettes. Toni had the most unfortunate position, facing the moon. Light beaded her skin like sweat as she listened to Amanda talk about whether or not she should break up with Boone, whom they'd referred to for months as The Hot Chiropractor, even after Amanda had started dating him.

The problem with Boone was that he was boring. "When he talks, my mind drifts," Amanda said. "I try to focus, but it's like trying to listen to my CPA, or to Miss Engler, my Pre-Calc teacher back in high school. I actually had to dig my nails into my arm to stop myself from falling asleep in her class. It was a first-thing-in-the-morning class, but still: there was something about her voice, droning like a bee, like the waah-waah grown-ups in the *Charlie Brown* specials. I would leave class with these gouges in my arm."

As the married one, Toni felt her life was shorter somehow than her friends' lives. She pictured herself as a squat succulent surrounded by ivies trailing their glossy stems over everything. Amanda's and Louise's years were broken into so many different chunks demarcated by who they were involved with at the time. Toni had one "relationship" before Nick, which hardly lasted a year, not to mention it was so long ago, and she'd been so young, that it didn't count in the way that her friends' adult relationships counted.

"Does it really matter that Boone is boring?" Louise said. "I mean, he's good-looking. And he's good in bed, right?"

In the dim light, Amanda's blush was only visible because she pressed her hands against her cheeks. In Toni's opinion, Amanda could have been a hand model. Her fingers were long and tendrilly and looked like something one would sculpt. Amanda said, "It's fine when he isn't talking."

"There are skills to deal with boring people," Louise said. "I can teach you. Seriously, I have the most boring patient ever. I've been honing my repertoire." Louise was a therapist. "And there are plenty of people in your life whom you can turn to for interesting conversation: me, Toni. Boone doesn't need to fulfill every need. This is the biggest cause for unhappiness: people expect their romantic partner to supply everything—stimulate them, soothe them in that fucked up Plato 'you complete me' way. It's delusional." Louise dropped beneath the water's surface. When she came up again, she said to Toni, "You don't expect Nick to fulfill all your needs, right?"

Toni manufactured a laugh. "Are you kidding?"

When she talked about Nick with her friends, she did so gingerly. She might admit, for instance, that Nick's slovenliness drove her crazy and that sometimes she asked him questions she already knew the answers to just to get some attention. But there was so much about marriage that she didn't tell them, wouldn't even know how to explain. Like the fact it had made her a suspicious person.

She was suspicious, for example, that Nick timed their fights to serve ulterior purposes. Last night he'd picked a fight with her at the end of the second day straight of record-breaking high temperatures. Their bedroom was the hottest room in the house, the most impervious to air-conditioning, and their home office was the coolest, with by far the prettiest night-time view—a skylight through which one could see a splash of stars. The couch was a pull-out bed, but tricky to pull out—you had to untangle the legs from zippered pockets. Toni lay in their bedroom alone, staring at the ceiling that badly needed repainting, and imagined Nick, if he wasn't sleeping soundly, looking instead at those strewn stars. Toni sweated, brooded, and contemplated the word "suspicious"—a word that implied both someone who suspects and a suspect.

It takes one to know one.

A bat fluttered overhead, gobbling up mosquitoes. The jerky, mechanical way they flew made them seem unnatural. "Human" was the word that came to Toni. Every time she went to see Boone for an adjustment (Toni introduced Amanda to Boone), after pressing his weight into her five or six times along various parts of her spine, neck, and hips, he said, "Stand up and give that a go." Then he watched Toni as she took a few steps across the room. She always felt self-conscious in this moment, but also, she felt a separation from her body. It was a vehicle she took out for a spin, and Boone understood more about how it worked than she did.

Amanda is ungrateful, Toni thought, disloyally. What one wanted in a partner is someone who understood one's body, how to soothe it, fix it, please it; not someone cunning and self-ish, someone who strategically picked fights like picking ripe loquats from a tree, who slept soundly while one irradiated and burned, so even a pool in the Arizona evening couldn't cool her off. "Interesting" was entirely overrated. Toni swallowed the rage she felt now not only towards her husband but also towards her best friend. But the sky felt wide and shocking, full of bats with meaty wings and strange, kitten-ish faces, and behind them, ag-gressive stars.

COMMON MISTAKES

HUMAN RESOURCES' WOOHOO INITIATIVE has hardly taken its first breath when eager-beaver Wendy Chase, one of the Curriculum Engineers, sends the company's first woohoo. She tags Barry Stevens, Lakshmi Patel, Martina Rodriguez, and Sibley Meyer-Banks, also Curriculum Engineers. The Woohoo commends Barry on his eye for details, Lakshmi on her willingness to pitch in, Martina for her dedication to always doing what's right for students, and Sibley for being an enthusiastic team player.

Soon, the Woohoo channel is flooded with woohoos from people all over the company. Each woohoo is accompanied by a supporting detail describing the woohoo'd individual's woohoo worthiness. I take notes.

At 11:45, the earliest time feasible, I walk over to Gigi's cubicle and say, "Get lunch with me?"

Gigi looks at me guardedly. "I brought a sandwich," she says.

"We can sit by the fountain. I can get a quesadilla at the food truck. Come on," I say. "I want to talk to you about something."

"Anne, I absolutely do not have time or energy to talk about 'us' right now."

I, of course, expected this response, so it is with a certain satisfaction that I say, immediately, "This has nothing to do with us! The last thing I want to talk about is us. This has to do with some observations I've made about our work environment."

Gigi narrows her eyes. "I also don't have time, or energy, to hear you bitch again about your job."

"Observations, not complaints," I clarify. "I'm interested in getting your thoughts about certain conclusions I've been drawing about what qualities this place values in women."

That hooks her. Gigi is even more attuned to the way the world shortchanges women than I am. Also, Gigi cannot resist an opportunity to give her opinion, which she will often do unsolicited, regarding, for instance, the bad economics of not packing one's lunch for work and procuring it instead at a food truck.

Reluctantly, she gathers her purse and her sandwich, which is exploding with alfalfa sprouts.

We sit on the concrete rim of the fountain, already hot from the morning sun. Gigi places, deliberately, her purse between us, so I flatten my paper on top of the purse and point to the "Happy Helpers" heading I've written on top.

"So, note the pattern of Wendy Chase's woohoos," I say. "See how she's woohooing Lakshmi for pitching in, Martina for her dedication to students, and Sibley for being an enthusiastic team player? Then there's Darren woohooing Ali for always stepping in to assist anyone struggling to complete a project on time? And Rosamund woohooing Kirsten for her positive attitude? And Kevin woohooing Paula for her generosity? See how the women are all being complimented for being nurturing mamas and cheerful second bananas?"

Gigi blinks at my notes. She chews a big bite of cucumbers, avocado, and sprouts. After swallowing, she takes a long drink from her water bottle. Then she says, "You've taken quite the inventory, haven't you? Is this what you did all morning?"

"No," I say, even though I know it's useless to lie to Gigi. She knows all about how once I get worked up about something, I struggle to let it go. She claims that if our time together were made into a pie chart, my rants would take up a Pacman-sized portion of that pie. According to Gigi, my rants are also indicative of all kinds of flaws in my cognition—that I have a poor attention span and a negative mindset. Gigi is on the Assessment team, mathematics to be precise, meaning she spends her days figuring out how to pinpoint flaws in other people's computations. A topic she will talk on and on about, if you let her, is how to write discriminating assessment items. A good distractor answer choice, she says, gives concrete information to teachers about where students' thinking is misguided, where they need further instruction. Gigi's self-described special talent, in fact, is coming up with these distractor choices, figuring out what common mistakes will tempt, even compel, test respondents toward the incorrect answer.

In the middle of the night, I've developed many theories about what it means that she's so adept at composing these red herrings, and what it means that I fell in love with and have lived for three and a half years with a woman whose special skillset is to come up with the perfect bad answers to lead one astray.

I've also pondered how proximity to someone who is good at spotting and then exploiting flaws in another's cognition has made me, through a kind of osmosis or close observation, adept at this myself. For instance, I know that my girlfriend is susceptible to opportunities to proffer her opinion, solicited or otherwise, particularly in the form of "constructive criticism."

The red herring I'm particularly susceptible to, I've decided, is unfairness. My most recent fixation, prior to the sexism embedded in my coworkers' woohoos, involves the bags of clothing Gigi's ex gave her when they last had lunch together. Tamara gave birth last year to twins and has officially given up on getting back to her pre-pregnant clothing size, so she gifted Gigi with various clothing items Gigi coveted and sometimes borrowed (stole) when they were still together, including a gorgeous, skimpy red dress that Gigi has a framed photograph of Tamara wearing. Yes, Gigi is in the photograph, too, as well as four other women. No, I am not particularly bothered that she has a photograph of Tamara in our house or that she's still friends with Tamara. The issue is that dress. Here's the thing: Gigi sees no problem with her wearing the dress, but she objects to me wearing it. On her, the dress has no significant meaning. But on me, the dress becomes representative of Tamara. Her explanation was about as comprehensible as her process for composing distractor choices on assessment tests. It made me think of one of our worst fights ever, when I asked Tamara for her mocha cheesecake recipe so I could make it for Gigi's birthday, and Gigi refused to eat it. Gigi acted as if my emailing Tamara for the recipe for her favorite dessert ever was weird overstepping on my part, instead of an expression of thoughtfulness and love. In the middle of the night, I have sometimes relived that evening, except instead of having it end with me sleeping on the couch, it ends with me force-feeding Gigi that cake in creamy forkfuls.

A few days ago, Gigi relented, and she took the dress, along with Tamara's other hand-me-downs, to the thrift store that benefits the local women's shelter.

But this didn't satisfy me. I believe she should have at least let me wear the dress one time before giving it away, and I say so again now as a sparrow swoops in fast to grab one of the sprouts from Gigi's sandwich that has fallen onto the concrete. I watch the bird drop the sprout and circle it, trying to assess how to swallow it.

Gigi shakes her head at me. "I told you I don't want to talk about us right now. You know I have to get that test ready for

Simon to green light by 6:00 today. I am sick of discussing that damn dress."

I explain again that I endured a social gathering at which she wore the dress, so she should have given me a turn, too.

Gigi looks at me like I'm one of the kids who picks what she calls throwaway distractors—answer choices that are so obviously wrong, all the choice can possibly reveal about a test taker is that she isn't even reading the questions, just randomly circling in bubbles. "Anne, you are impossible to please," she says, through gritted teeth. "I did what you wanted. I took the clothes to the shelter. Instead of haranguing me about the dress, you should be appreciative that I made a sacrifice purely to appease you."

There are times when I feel like I'm dating my mother. When Gigi looks at me in that particular bleak way, I can hear my mother say, don't roll your eyes at me, young lady. Being made to feel petulant was so lonely. I remember as a teenager imagining I would one day meet someone who appreciated and understood me; I remember believing this person was out there, waiting for me to materialize.

SPORES

MOST OF THE WOMEN AT THE GYM, I CAN tell by a quick glance I wouldn't like them. They wear sleek ponytails or precious braids. They look like store displays in their expensive, trendy workout clothes. Tops that crisscross their backs like shoelaces. Shoes that coordinate with those tops. They log hours on treadmills and ellipticals. If they do lift weights, they hover around the dainty dumbbells near the physio balls—the soft, colored dumbbells that evoke '80s Jazzercise leotards. The dumbbells remind me of plastic dinosaurs the dentist puts in my kid's dental-visit goodie bag. But not Sheila. Well, I don't actually know her name; Sheila is just what I call her in my head. Sheila lifts the bulky, black dumbbells that the men lift. Sheila comes to the gym in T-shirts she probably got for free. One of them is a faded red that is almost pink. It reads, "Fred's Dry Cleaning." I have imagined long conversations between us, Sheila in that dry cleaning shirt—the two of us sipping protein smoothies at the gym café.

The only interaction I've ever had with Sheila is when some woman—one of the thin, pony-tailed, fancy-workout-clothes chicks—left the exercise bike without wiping it down. Hard to believe that such a small person would exude so much sweat; it's a reminder that the human body is composed of more than sixty percent water. The banana seat of the bike was so wet that it reflected the halogen ceiling lights. In a different context it might have been pretty, like an Impressionist painting where the orange ball of a sun is mirrored in the ocean. I had forgotten, as usual, to bring my gym towel, so I looked at the seat and said, dejectedly, "Gross." Sheila, standing on the other side of the bike, looked at it, agreed "Gross," and handed me her towel. Like the dry cleaning shirt, the towel was worn to the nub. I wiped off the seat, said, "Thanks," and handed it back to her. In that brief exchange, I felt a meeting of the minds, a mutual disdain for these lithe, sweaty bimbos with their dyed eyelashes. With their yoga pants that are weirdly expensive in the way fancy jeans are expensive because they flatter their asses. Fuck them all, was what our eyes communicated to each other, before Sheila slung her ratty towel over her shoulder and I mounted the now non-gleaming bike.

The first thing my husband says when I tell him about Sheila as we drive out of the gym parking lot is "Sheila? Why Sheila?" Then, "Why don't you just ask if she'd like to get coffee or something?"

"She'd think I was a weirdo. Would you ask a guy you don't know out for coffee?"

"No," Phillip says, "But one, *I* have friends, and two, going out for coffee is not a thing men do together."

"I see plenty of men together in coffee shops."

Phillip yells, "Go! Go! You could have made that light."

"I didn't want to make that light."

"Those men are probably gay," Phillip says.

While we sit at the red light, I study my husband's profile. He is, I estimate, about forty percent better looking than when I married him. The creases that line his face make him more beautiful somehow, like a drawing that an artist has come back to again and again, adding little details, obsessing over.

Phillip says, "I still don't understand why you and Theresa don't hang out anymore."

"I've told you a million times: we don't have anything in common. It was a superficial friendship. I feel like she doesn't really like me or even know me, for that matter."

"Well, you're not exactly easy to get to know. Green light."

Phillip isn't trying to hurt me. Despite his social skills, he tends to make by my estimation poor observations: "Needs salt." Or "That skirt isn't flattering." And I know I worry him, and Allie worries him, or more precisely, Allie's similarity to me worries him. "She's introverted," he'll say, like it's a character defect, instead of a personality trait. Then he'll look at me in this accusatory way, and I know he's picturing Allie's social awkwardness like it's a genetic trait on one of those Punnett squares. The truth is, Allie is a blend of both of us, my shyness merged with Phillip's flat-footed, damn-the-torpedoes conversational style. Once on the playground, when Allie was about four, another girl introduced herself to Allie as "Cinderella." Allie folded her arms and said, "That's ridiculous."

I've pointed out to Phillip that introversion is preferred over extroversion in plenty of cultures, like Finland and Sweden and China, for instance, that it's not intrinsically a deficit. But then last week at the end-of-year teacher-parent conference, Allie's teacher Lorraine presented a long checklist tracking Allie's developmental progress. Lorraine had checked "mastered" for every item on the list except one: participates in group discussions. In that row Lorraine had checked the "not yet developed" box. Lorraine elaborated: "Allie has yet to speak when we're in circle. She's so bright and so intuitive. I hope that in time she'll gain the confidence to take on more of a leadership role in the classroom."

"Only in America," I said to Phillip in the parking lot. "No way is wanting to perform for an audience a developmental skill teachers in Finland are checking off for their students."

"I think it's nice that schools are concerned with the whole development of the child," Phillip said.

Now I say, "I'm plenty easy to get to know with the right kind of person."

Phillip laughs. Then he gets serious. "No one is ever going to live up to Helene. But friendships are like pizza. Some are better than others, sure, but a frozen pizza is better than no pizza."

This is the same metaphor Phillip has used for sex on several occasions, and yes, I recognize its lack of originality, though likening me to "frozen pizza" makes the metaphor more sinister.

"Don't," I say. For the rest of the five-minute drive, we're silent. One thing I appreciate about driving is it forces one to concentrate. I can't think about Helene when I'm looking out for pedestrians or the Volkswagen in front of me signaling or that weird, too fast yellow light at Larkin and Clay. I see things—a stringy-haired woman in a blue cardigan standing at the crosswalk, holding her daughter's hand, the girl about Allie's age. The images wipe away, scribbles on a whiteboard.

When I drop Phillip off outside his office, he hesitates. Then he says, "Artichokes for dinner?"

"Sure."

It's like that curt exchange with Sheila at the gym. Except this is my husband.

—

When we sit down for dinner, Phillip asks Allie about her day at camp. What was her favorite part of the day? What was her least favorite part of the day? These are the questions Phillip asks Allie every evening. They're as routine as making sure she brushes her teeth. The problem with "How was your day?" is that it begets paltry, one-word answers like "Fine." It's not a conversation starter.

Allie says, "My least favorite part of the day was lunch. Hot dogs and carrot sticks. My favorite part: playing chess with Thunder."

"Which one is Thunder?" Phillip says. "The viper?"

"Thunder is a kangaroo rat," I say. "He's always been a kangaroo rat."

According to Allie, Silver has always been a viper, but I distinctly remember that in the beginning, when Silver was the only imaginary friend she talked about, he was a dog. Allie will argue me to the death that I'm wrong, though.

"Who won?" Phillip says.

"Thunder," Allie says, "But that's only because I let him win."

"That reminds me," Phillip says, "has Mom told you about her new friend, Sheila?" He tries to suppress his smile.

"You're so amusing," I say, in a haughty British accent, because Allie is there. But my eyes communicate to him, You're an asshole.

Phillip thinks like an engineer: every problem has a solution. He's a human version of those electric paddles EM technicians press to one's chest to jumpstart the heart. He doesn't know what to do with problems that can't be fixed. Grief counselling was his idea, but I quit after three weeks, because everyone in that group was so competitive about their relative losses. They'd lost spouses, they'd lost children: how was losing a best friend supposed to compare? It was tragedy one-upmanship. Partly just to see their expressions, I was tempted to say, Hey, I'd trade my husband to have her back. The truth is there are moments when I think I would do exactly that.

Helene had had a theory about reincarnation, that the soul didn't survive intact, that it didn't get dropped neatly into some new body package, like scooping filling into a new pie shell. Helene figured at the moment of death, different fragments of you flew out like spores and attached to random people: this bystander walking down Ninth Avenue would get her terrible posture (Helene lamented that she looked like a pelican); this six-year-old feeding coins into the snack machine would get her acute sense of smell. She'd been kidding, but now I find myself looking for scraps of Helene wherever I go. On the bus, I see a woman scrambling through her purse, or a teenager twisting her hair around her finger, or an old man crossing his ankles in a particular way. Sheila doesn't resemble Helene at all—she's stocky and muscular, not tall and stooped—but a certain disdainful way she has of looking not at, but through, those color-coordinated gym bunnies reminds me of Helene.

Allie leans back into her chair so that it's balanced on only the back two legs and says, "Who's Sheila?"

You can always tell from Allie's physical posture whether

she likes what's for dinner. Spaghetti with meatballs, and she's bent over her plate. Artichokes, Brussels sprouts, beets, and she's falling out of her chair or hugging her knees against her chest or looking for the cat.

"Sit properly and eat your dinner," I say.

She replants the chair, repeats the question.

"She's a woman from the gym," I say.

"So you exercise together?" she says.

"Not exactly," I say.

"What do you do together?" Allie says.

I look to Phillip, but he's like Allie with spaghetti, his eyes focused on his plate.

"Honestly," I say, "I don't know her. She leant me a towel once. I just think that I might like to be friends with her. But I'm not sure how to go about it. Making friends is hard for adults too."

Allie puts her hand on mine, smiles tenderly at me. Then she says, "Can I have dessert?"

—

I've been complaining to Phillip for years that the T-shirts I sleep in have a woody smell—not gross exactly, but off-putting. If I burrow under the sheets at night, the odor is overwhelming, like I'm sleeping in a twig-constructed nest bedded with sawdust. I theorized that the dresser drawers were responsible somehow, only if that were true, shouldn't Phillip's T-shirts smell like wood too? They didn't. I sniffed him night after night. Never did he smell like wood.

Then I come across this blog about living a minimalist lifestyle, about how all these people decluttered their homes, getting rid of thousands of possessions, and what they learned about themselves in the process. One guy calculated that the cheaply priced things he got rid of added up to something like ten thousand dollars. A woman realized she'd been buying clothes she didn't need in an effort to feel better about her body. So she stopped buying clothes and took up running instead.

What I learn as I empty out my dresser drawers and discard the clothes I no longer wear is that one, I have a ridiculous number of T-shirts I've never worn, not even once, and two, the source of the woody smell I've been complaining about is a pretty blue sachet filled with dried herbs and cedar. A gift from Helene. The sachet wasn't even hidden beneath all those shirts. It was visible, but I never noticed it. And now that I do see it, I feel both foolish and sad. I hold the sachet up in the air by its ribbon like dangling a mouse by its tail.

"How is it possible I never considered this sachet?" I say to Phillip, who is lying in bed reading a nonfiction book about robots.

"So throw it away."

"Helene gave it to me."

Phillip looks at me, and I see the different emotions flicker across his face, competing for ascendancy: pity, concern, but also his familiar frustration when I'm being irrational. Phillip doesn't get why I make things, in his words, "needlessly complicated." When Allie's teacher sent the class home with incoherent directions about how to write their research reports on an animal of their choosing, Phillip said, "Just email her." When I continued raging about her nonsense prompt, he said, "Fine, I'll email Lorraine!" He simply wanted Allie to get started on researching the black mamba (because of course, Allie had chosen a viper). He couldn't understand the gratification (and I concede, it's a peculiar gratification, hard to appreciate) of finding yet more evidence of inept authority in action. God as a halfwit sadist, human beings scrambling for a light switch in the pitch black.

"So keep it," he says.

"But it smells like a sawmill."

Phillip disappears—I imagine he's finally gone to call the people in the white van, with the butterfly nets—but a minute later he's back with a freezer bag, with a smaller Ziploc sandwich bag inside it. "Okay, so put it in this and seal them both. It'll lock in the smell."

Sure enough, when I sniff the freezer bag, there's no woody smell. The sachet inside the bags reminds me of the Invisible Woman my parents got me at the Natural History Museum gift shop on a trip we once took to New York. Her plastic body was transparent, but you could see all her organs inside.

"So I have a proposal," says my husband. "You ask this woman Sheila for coffee—heck, you ask her for her real name, and I'll go down on you every day for a week."

I must look horrified, because Phillip immediately backtracks. "Bad idea? Okay, how about I take you to that ballet you want to see? That swan one?"

"You loathe ballet."

It was Phillip's idea that I join the gym after I quit the grief counselling group. Something about how I needed the endorphins. I wonder now if he was also hoping I'd make a friend. I look at my husband, who doesn't respond to my comment other than to grimace, and I think about a night eleven years ago, when I was at The Spitball with Helene. She was trying to get me to approach a guy at the bar she claimed was checking me out. "He's cute! Go talk to him. Go buy him a drink," she said, and I kept shaking my head. Not just because the idea of approaching a stranger, even one who was eyeing me, made my limbs feel gummy, but also because at the time I couldn't picture myself with any man other than my ex, Geoffrey. I didn't expect or even want to get back together with him. The best way I can think to explain it is that Geoffrey, even in his absence, felt as natural and familiar as my own skull. I am a woman who doesn't wear make-up other than lipstick. I've never even temporarily colored my hair. Helene knew all of this, so finally she said, "Okay, if you get that dude's number, you can wear my puffer vest again." (This was a glorious, slate-gray vest I had been banned from wearing, after once spilling dessert wine on the breast). "Fuck it, you can have the vest! Now go talk to him," and Helene had actually shoved the small of my back, propelling me towards the guy at the bar who was indeed objectively cute, though forty percent less so than he is now.

DELUXE SCRABBLE

FOR MOTHER'S DAY, I BUY MYSELF THE Deluxe Scrabble that comes with a lazy Susan. I delete the Amazon confirmation from my inbox because Harry will freak if he realizes I spent $119 on a board game no one in our family besides me will play. It comes in a blue box with a cream-colored border, reminding me of the fancy placemats we had when I was a kid, and the fancy cloth napkins, each a different color. My mother would fold them into pretty shapes that looked like half-peeled bananas. My mother used to starch and iron those napkins. In contrast, my napkins are wrinkled around the edges. When Harry folds and puts away laundry, he mixes those napkins up with the tea towels. He and our son, Noah, are seemingly indifferent to the distinctions and will pull out whatever's on top of the stack and use it to wipe their greasy hands during meals.

When I was a kid, I had this friend named Sunshine. Sunshine's house was filthy, and if I walked barefoot on her family's tile floors, the soles of my feet would turn gray-black. Always there was a stray grape or blueberry on the floor in the kitchen or the papery red husk of an onion, sometimes a grocery receipt, a twisty tie, a hairpin. But I spent nearly every day of the summer at Sunshine's house because her mother Desiree was what people in those days called a housewife, and she loved games. The three of us, Sunshine, Desiree, and me, would play games for hours at a time: Yahtzee, dominoes, Sorry, and, my favorite, Scrabble.

I thought Desiree was the most beautiful name I'd ever heard. She insisted I call her Desiree, whereas my mother went by "Mrs. Brock." It's a formality she maintained. She never told Harry to call her Livia, so he avoided calling her anything at all, which made dinners with my mother awkward, Harry waiting until he could look her in the eye to address her. "It's too bizarre to call my mother-in-law of fifteen years 'Mrs. Brock!'" he used to complain.

The few times Sunshine visited my house, I felt self-conscious about how formal everything was. I saw it all through her eyes: it was like sinking into an underwater world. Without really speaking aloud why, the two of us soon settled into a routine of spending all our time together at Sunshine's house.

After we played a game of Scrabble, Desiree and Sunshine and I would look at the completed board and pick out our favorite words, the coolest words, not the ones that scored the most points. I remember feeling proud when Desiree chose my word "banshee." She maintained it was worth getting fewer points, or even wasting an "s," if you could spell something interesting like "fiasco," or line your word right on top of another word, so the two words looked like prone lovers, or neat shelves. "That's so elegant," Desiree would say, and I realized that despite her sticky house she embodied an elegance materially different from my mother's napkin folding.

Desiree taught me that being good at Scrabble was all about memorizing the two-letter words. "Cheating," is what Harry calls those words. Nothing will annoy him more than when I admit I don't know what "xi" means, but I know it's a word.

Some summer mornings when I entered the kitchen through the screened door in Sunshine's garage, I was greeted by the warm, burnt-sugar scent of homemade blueberry crumb cake. Those were the best days. Desiree had no rules about portion size or the number of servings we were allowed to eat, or how close it was to dinner time. Sometimes we polished off an entire cake, playing round after round after round.

But eventually, after a honeymoon of perfect days, there came days when Desiree was distant or a little short-tempered or just strange. The first time, I remember there weren't more than a few words on the Scrabble board when Desiree pushed herself up from the table and said, "I'm done." She disappeared down the hallway that led to her bedroom, and we didn't see her again that day. I'd been the last one to play before she quit: "ice." I remember the word because, ridiculously, I wondered if I'd disappointed her, if I was the reason she abandoned us.

I had always been a little scared of Sunshine's dad. In fact, I tried to keep an eye on the clock in the afternoons to make sure I left before he returned home from work. He seemed made of stone, or encased in stone, like it might take a pickax to chisel him out. He didn't seem like the kind of man who'd have a daughter named Sunshine.

Once in a while, though, he'd come home smiling and laughing. His cheeks seemed rosy on those days, his hair fluffier. The day that Desiree said she was done was one of those days. I stayed at Sunshine's house late into the afternoon because her mother had already abandoned her, and I didn't want to do the same.

When Sunshine's dad walked into the kitchen, leaving his umbrella in the garage to dry—it had rained all afternoon—he patted her on the head like she was a dog. "How are my girls?" he said, and for a moment, I thought he meant me and Sunshine. Then he said, "Where's Dez?"

I remember wincing, to hear Desiree's beautiful name chopped into something that sounded like a pill you'd pop in a glass of water, which would make the water cloud and fizz. But also, it made me think about how my father always called my mother "Your mother," as in, "Where's your mother?" As if she had no name or independent identity aside from that role, her production of us, her folding of napkins into their lovely, stiff shapes.

"She's in the bedroom," Sunshine said, and her father nodded and said, "Will you hang up my coat, Princess?"

Funny: the things one does and doesn't remember. I remember his coat, the color of toast, lined in red plaid, and I remember noticing, for the first time, the coat-hooks on the wall of the foyer, not hooks at all, but round like doorknobs. But I don't remember the name of Sunshine's father. I don't remember why he frightened me, though I certainly remember watching the kitchen clock to see if it was getting close to 5:00, and I remember how much I wished that clock was in my bedroom. It was one of those cat-shaped clocks with a long tail and eyes that slid from left to right, like the cat was thinking, weighing possibilities. I wondered: if I could see all that cat saw when I wasn't at Sunshine's house, would I understand her parents any better? Would I understand my own?

When Sunshine's father disappeared into her parents' bedroom, Sunshine suggested we go outside and look for frogs. There were almost always frogs in the grass after a good rain. Some of them were as small as Scrabble tiles. Sunshine said they fell from the sky. That didn't make any sense to me, but I couldn't offer up a better explanation of where they'd come from. When we placed them on our palms, the frogs peed, but we didn't mind. They were so delicate. They tickled our skin.

I imagined back then that whatever was going on with Desiree on the days that she retreated from us was of soap opera proportions. She watched *Days of Our Lives*, which was on in the background for an hour each day. Usually, we played something kind of brainless during *Days* so that she wouldn't miss anything important—new developments about the Salem Strangler or various love affairs. When she clicked on the television, Desiree would say, "I know it's dumb." Or, "It's my one vice." I don't think I had any particular plot in mind when Desiree hid out in her bedroom all day, but I imagined her bedroom as dark and kind of sinister. I pictured Desiree in a satin nightgown, something sexy as opposed to the frilly, fuzzy nightgowns my mother wore.

When Sunshine and I went back inside and washed our hands after handling frogs, there was a frozen pizza on the kitchen counter, along with a sticky note that read, "For you and Millie. You can watch a movie." I knew the tiny, neat print was Sunshine's dad's handwriting because I knew Desiree's handwriting from her keeping score. Her handwriting was sloppy, like her kitchen floor. Her handwriting took up space.

"You like pepperoni, right?" Sunshine asked me, but even though I did, I was seized with an urgent desire to leave. It was as if that dark, sinister bedroom had reached out to encase everything else. Even the cat clock on the wall, the clock I'd always loved, seemed menacing instead of vigilant. The ticking noise its tail made was signaling to me go, go, go.

"I promised I'd be home for dinner," I said.

Sunshine looked at me, surprised and then unsurprised. It was as if my defection was something she'd been waiting for: like those characters on *Days* when they receive some awful but long-anticipated news.

That same summer, my mother's little Yorkshire terrier, Boswell, who had a face like a Muppet, died. He was fourteen. She earnestly referred to him as her "firstborn," as though he had come into this world the same route I had. But the way she loved him was starkly different from the way she loved me. She dressed both of us up in ridiculous, uncomfortable outfits, and she tried tirelessly to train us to obey, but she doted on that dog. Practically the only time I saw my mother smile was when Boswell sat on her lap, and she scratched him behind his ears. When I was really little, I was so jealous of Boswell that I schemed about ways to murder him.

But Boswell's death taught me that murdering him when I was younger wouldn't have made my mother dote on me more. I was the one who found him that June morning, his legs stretched out stiffly, so he looked like a footstool tipped over on its side. "Mom!" I'd called, though I usually called her Mother. She cried when she saw him, but when I said, "Poor Boswell" and tried to hug her, she shook her head and crossed her arms protectively. In bed that night I cried, not because I felt sad about Boswell particularly—he'd always ignored me, except when I was near the cabinet where my mother kept a cookie jar of dog biscuits, and then he'd whine and nose the back of my legs. I cried because I kept visualizing my mother's wet, cold eyes. I was convinced she blamed me for finding him.

One evening when I returned home from Sunshine's house, my mother said at dinner, "I don't know that I like you spending every day at that girl's house. I bet her mother would like some peace and quiet." With her long dark hair and erect posture, my mother reminded me of Morticia Addams, but with less charm.

When I told her that Desiree played board games with us, my mother raised her eyebrows, but said nothing more.

This was sometime after Desiree abandoned Sunshine and me in the middle of that Scrabble game in which I played "ice." It was also after the game of Scrabble in which Sunshine tried to play "passion," but she spelled it wrong, and Desiree laughed and said, "Passion with one lonely 's.' That's hilarious." Sunshine had said, "Don't make fun of me." She'd crossed her arms and sulked. Desiree had looked startled. "Oh, hon, I wasn't making fun of you." She'd leaned over and kissed Sunshine on her head. "You are the most important thing in the world to me." Not long after that, though, Desiree said she didn't feel good and was going to take a bath. She slid her remaining tiles back into the black pouch.

I believe I told my mother about Desiree playing games with us to defend myself—to clarify that I wasn't imposing—but once I said it, I thought about those two abandoned games and I wondered if maybe my mother was right.

It certainly didn't occur to me that anything about that exchange could be upsetting to my mother. I'd forgotten all about it when my father knocked on my bedroom door later that night, sat on my bed, and said, "Hey, Chicken: you made your mother feel bad."

That summer, I kept oscillating between having a grandiose sense of power and feeling utterly insignificant. As an example of the first, I felt responsible for Boswell's death, because years ago, I'd fantasized poisoning him. When my mother looked at me with her red, teary eyes, she'd seemed to accuse my jealous, seven-year-old self. On the other hand, I was shocked that anything I could say would wound her. I had no idea what my father was even talking about that night. That was long before I was trained in couples counseling, as well as in required so-called personal development classes at work, to take ownership of my feelings and to separate my feelings from facts. Back then, I had no qualms with the idea that other people, my mother especially, could be responsible for my feelings, but the reverse was unfathomable. And why wouldn't it be? My mother had trained me to raise my hand if I needed to speak to her and to wait to be called on. This wasn't just for occasions on which she had company and so to prevent my interrupting conversation. My mother explained that she startled easily and that children were abrupt.

Even when my father explained himself, I just stared at him.

Then he said, as he had several times over the years, "Your

mother had a rough childhood. It follows her, you know?" I didn't know. My father never elaborated on this statement. I pictured a hooded, shadowy figure, like a jailer, standing in the corner, its eyes tracking my mother.

Sunshine's birthday was on the solstice. "The longest, hottest day of the year," Desiree said as she brought out a white-frosted cake covered in rainbow sprinkles.

For the occasion, Sunshine's father had set out a blue tarp and covered it in soapy water so that if we ran and leaped onto it, we slid all the way across. He'd put out buckets of water and blue sponges that Sunshine and her cousins threw at each other.

It was a family birthday party, except for me. That could have been awkward, especially since I didn't know Sunshine's cousins, and Alexandra in particular was intimidating, with her purple eyeliner and feathery bangs. But Desiree put her arm around me and said, "This is Millie. Millie's honorary family." It's hard to describe how special that made me feel. It made me want to cry.

My memory, as noted, is unreliable: it's like a piece of linen that moths have gotten to, full of lacy holes. But just today, when I was sitting by myself at our dining room table (Noah at soccer practice, Harry who-the-fuck knows where), playing myself at Scrabble (Millie against Amelia, no one has called me "Millie" for at least fifteen years), that whole party unfurled in my mind. I was arranging the letters in Millie's rack—HORN, HONOR, HOAR—and then I realized I could use them all if I played on the Y. Once that clicked, the memory clicked as well, like a Scrabble tile locking into a slot. I saw the wet blue tarp, I heard the smack and slide of bodies, I felt Desiree's warm arm around my shoulder.

I remembered how Sunshine said my present was the prettiest of the bunch—shiny rose-colored paper wrapped in a fancy white bow that reminded me of a sea anemone. The wrapping was pretty, I suppose, but the word that came to my mind was *gaudy*. My mother wrapped it. She picked out Sunshine's gift, too. I had wanted to buy Sunshine a bracelet kit I'd seen at Target, but from across our dining room table, my mother had frowned. She said, "She's your best friend. Let's get her something special."

My mother perked up then. She said we'd make a day of it. She'd take me to lunch at that restaurant that does the tea service with the platters of little sandwiches with their crusts cut off and mini quiches and pastries, where your tea is served with a bowl full of sparkling sugar cubes. She said, "Doesn't that sound fun?" My father smiled. He gave me a pointed glance. I thought of poor little Boswell when my mother tried to trick him to get inside his dog carrier to go to the vet. She'd place a dog biscuit all the way in the back. Boswell knew it was a trick. He'd look at the treat, then look at my mother and whimper.

That's how I ended up giving Sunshine a Precious Moments figurine of two girls holding hands. The base on which the girls stood read, "Two Friends, One Heart."

When Sunshine lifted the figurine from the box, her cousin Alexandra smirked. One of Sunshine's aunts said, "That's just darling."

It was probably a hundred degrees outside, but I was mostly sweating from embarrassment.

Sunshine was sweet about it. She thanked me and gave me a hug. Maybe she really did like the figurine, but that wasn't the point.

The point was I had been too worried about my mother's feelings to insist on picking out my best friend's birthday gift. Standing there in my dripping swimsuit in Sunshine's yard, I hated my mother.

That evening, when my mother asked what Sunshine thought of her gift, I said, "She liked it." I even smiled at my mother. But I wasn't really seeing my mother at all. I was imagining Desiree across the table from me—Desiree, my honorary mother. I was thinking how she loved me like I was her own daughter; how she loved me in a way my own mother was incapable of.

The following March, right before I turned twelve, though, that illusion was shattered when Sunshine and Desiree moved to Montana. As they got into their packed station wagon, my and Sunshine's faces wet with tears, Desiree spoke only of my and

Sunshine's friendship: "You'll write each other letters. You'll talk on the phone. Distance will make your friendship all the more special, you'll see."

Distance didn't.

And it comes to me today, this strange, sad, lonely Mother's Day—a holiday that my husband and son didn't even remember this morning, because let's face it, it's stupid, created by Hallmark to sell cards; a holiday my own mother always disdained, though ironically, this is the first anniversary of her death—that here's another meaning for "honorary": a family member that only contingently belongs.

A TEST I KNEW
I COULD PASS

THIS NEWSBOY-HAT-WEARING GUY HAL told my friend Mallory that he'd like to dictate her tastes. Quote: "Don't misunderstand, Love. You're golden, but your aesthetics are shite." We were at Mallory's stepbrother Kevin's housewarming party. Barely twenty-four, already Kevin owned a house. Fancy too. Mallory and I had been imagining how we'd spend half the upcoming summer lounging around Kevin's pool, drinking pretty cocktails, when Hal made his offer. Mallory said, "You're not even British. And what is this? *Pygmalion*?" which is why once Mallory went outside to find Kevin, Hal reluctantly talked to me.

He was cute in a blurry way, like a sketch I'd smudged with my thumb.

"How do you know Kevin?" I asked, and it turned out they played in the same soccer league, only Hal called it football. When he said, "No, British football," I understood that was the whole point: that's probably why he played soccer in the first place, so he could go around calling it football. Like he called the potato chips we were eating "crisps." But I'm not Mallory: I'm completely willing to be educated, to have my tastes and vocabulary re-shaped.

The weekend before, Mallory and I had drawn vision trees on butcher paper. Some of my leaves had been concrete objectives, like "get a boyfriend," but others more abstract, like "be less wishy-washy." I'd never admit it to Mallory, but in truth, I'm ambivalent about Neil Diamond, who Mallory says is a dream, or was, in the '70s. I'm ambivalent about a lot of things Mallory believes we both love, like fried calamari, clove cigarettes, and Scottish Fold cats.

"Hand me a crisp," I said to Hal, and a flicker of interest ignited in Hal's eyes. I pictured myself as a damp blob of clay, spinning on a potter's wheel.

He invited me over to his apartment to watch Andy Warhol's *Empire*. He told me to dress comfortably and bring a snack to share, "only nothing that smells too weird," instructions I spent several hours deconstructing. Eventually, I settled on a flannel shirt and jeans, and a spinach cheese dip with a sliced baguette.

I don't know how many minutes passed as the light on the white screen slowly, slowly shifted until the Empire State Building emerged like an image being developed on photographic paper. Or how many more minutes passed before I asked, "So is anything going to happen in this movie?" But from the beginning, time felt vast, as though the carbon and other elements in the baguette I was quickly devouring were already helping form new eyeball cells to replace the cells the film was exhausting.

"The day is happening," Hal said.

I thought he meant our day, the time we were spending together, so I tried to subtly scoot closer to him on the sofa. But then Hal explained that the film consisted of eight hours of slow-motion footage. "The characters are the building, light, and, most importantly, time."

I stared at Hal, trying to figure out not whether I was being tested—obviously this was a test—but rather, the terms of the test. My capacity for boredom? My gullibility? I thought of the famous "Prisoners and Guards" case study Mallory and I had learned about in our psychology class. The study's subjects: the undergrads assigned to be guards. The study's focus: the corruptibility intrinsic to power. How long would it take these students to turn into sadists, to inflict, without wincing, electric shocks on the prisoners (who were only pretending to be hurt, but the guards had no way of knowing that)? What defect of mine was Hal assessing?

Because if what he was interested in was my willingness to improve myself, that's a test I knew I could pass.

I thought about how Ryan, my ex-boyfriend, had broken up with me. Well, I'd thought he was my boyfriend; I doubt Ryan would accept that title. We were having lunch. I was eating an egg salad sandwich. I was chewing, feeling happy that I was comfortable enough with Ryan to eat something weird and gross like an egg salad sandwich. Here's what he said: "It's not me, it's you." Then he laughed, and said, "Just kidding." For a mortifying minute, I wanted to ask what, exactly, he was kidding about—breaking up with me, or turning our breakup into some harsh punchline to relay to his friends? I felt a flash of relief when I thought it was the former.

Before he walked away, leaving me to finish my sandwich alone, he said, "Seriously, I don't know how you can eat that. It's disgusting." He wrinkled his nose at me. You are what you eat, I thought.

When I returned from Hal's bathroom, I said, "Did I miss anything?"

He didn't return my smile.

When the Empire State Building disappeared from the screen, I said that while the movie certainly felt slow, I was shocked by how quickly time had passed. "Maybe I was asleep with my eyes open?"

Hal looked at me as though I was as useless as the bit of string a Grinch cons a Hoobub into purchasing in a Seuss story I read recently to my little stepsister. Then he explained that what we'd watched was a one-hour bootlegged cut. You can't watch the film in its entirety unless the MOMA decides to show it.

I said, "Watching one hour of an eight-hour film is stupid, isn't it? Undermines the whole point?"

Hal smiled, said, "Very good." Then he tossed me a sea salt truffle, a reward, as though I was a dog that had sat on command.

The chocolate was, I felt certain, the best I'd ever tasted.

ABUSE AND OTHER WORDS MY MOTHER AND I DISAGREE ABOUT

MY MOTHER ACTS LIKE THE CONFLICT BE-tween her and me is semantic, rather than due to her crappy parenting. For instance, when I try to talk to her about how when I was a kid and she was pissed at me, or simply found me irritating and noisy, she would make me sit in the garage by myself for hours (pitch dark, smelling like rancid milk). She says, "It's ridiculous to call that 'abuse'! I never laid a hand on you. Your generation is much too loosey-goosey with words."

Which makes me smile—maddening as my mother is, the way she'll let fly some phrase like "loosey-goosey," as if she's a fifties housewife in a flowered apron, kills me.

So I press her. I want to know what other words she takes umbrage with.

She gives me a look to confirm that I'm not messing with her (my mother and I have minimal trust in each other), and says, "All right, what about gender? In my day, gender was a concrete thing that you just were. You all act as if it's a costume you can just throw on. 'Today I'm feeling like a girl.' Gender is not something you feel!"

"Says the woman who tells me I ought to make an effort to look more feminine," I say. "And what about your birthday twin?"

My mother hates it when I call David Bowie her birthday twin, though it is true they share the same birthday—same year as well as the same date. I realized this only after he died, and weirdly, this fact prompted me to call her when I heard the news. I took Bowie's death hard. What my mother said: "You didn't even know the man. It makes no sense to be so sad."

Impossible to explain to her that as a kid, I felt more seen by David Bowie than I did by my own mother. Those long, dark hours in the garage, Bowie was who kept me company. I sang "Life on Mars?" to myself and the crickets.

On the phone that evening, I repeated "saddening bore" over and over until my mother said, "Finis!"

Now she says, "His songs are nonsense."

"And what do you mean by nonsense?"

My mother looks at me, to verify that I'm not fucking with her, and apparently decides instead I'm a moron. She twirls one hand in the air, conveying dismissal. "Poppycock. Balderdash," she says, and again my irritation at her dissolves in the face of her words. The fifties housewife with the apron morphs into some

Victorian lord with a hooked, disdainful nose and a burgundy velvet smoking jacket.

Sometimes I think my mother and I would finally get along if, instead of trying to explain ourselves to each other, we just sat across a table and occasionally emitted single words: "Starship," "pernicious," "grasshopper."

TAB IS SAD

DORIAN SITS ON HER FRONT STOOP, WAIT-
ing for her friend Liz to pick her up so they can carpool to
Dorian's ex-girlfriend Claudia's pre-engagement party. When
Dorian got the invitation in the mail, a red envelope lettered by
Claudia's loopy, girlish handwriting, she thought there'd been
some kind of proofreading error. Like the silver flask in Dorian's
purse which she's filled to the brim with what Claudia calls
hooch. (Claudia is from Kentucky and has certain Kentucky ec-
centricities, including a penchant for ridiculous hats). The flask
is a Christmas present Claudia gave Dorian two years ago and
had engraved with Dorian's initials—DBJ—but that the en-
graver, for understandable reasons, fucked up, so instead it said
PBJ. Claudia didn't notice the mistake until Dorian pointed it
out, and then was close to tears; calming Claudia down required
work. But eventually the flask became a joke between them—before going to a baseball game, Claudia would say, "Make sure you
bring the peanut-butter-and-jelly"—and Dorian intends to produce the flask at some maximally opportune time in the next six
hours, and thereby fill Claudia with regret.

Claudia is pre-engaging herself (as ridiculous as celebrating a declaration that one intends to, in the future, quit drinking, but not yet) to a woman named Tab. A person named Tab, Dorian corrects herself. A non-binary individual named Tab. The only other instance Dorian has encountered the name Tab is in a beginning-readers story called *Tab and Mac*, in which a cat named Tab eats his mouse friend Mac when he wakes from a nap to find that Mac ate the ham in his food bowl. He's hungry and grumpy, and, well, he's a cat. The final image shows Tab suffering from remorse. A tear falls from his eye, and the text reads, "Tab is sad."

The kids Dorian tutors at the elementary school love that story. They laugh and laugh. Dorian wonders sometimes what it says about humans that the youngest among them find humor in friends eating their friends. To Dorian, the book is tragic—so tragic that she can barely stand to read it. She wants a *deus-ex-machina* intervention, like in the version of *Little Red Riding Hood* she also reads them. The huntsman cuts open the big bad wolf with an ax, and Little Red and the Grandmother spring out of his body, intact. She confessed to one kid, Bennie, her wish that Tab would eject a live, whole Mac from his throat like a hairball, and that mouse and cat would reconcile. Bennie looked at her with surprise, his large brown eyes pitying, and said, "But, Ms. James, that wouldn't be realistic."

Dorian assumed at the time that Bennie was referring to the impossibility of regurgitating a devoured meal whole, but now she wonders if he could have meant the impossibility of Mac being so forgiving. The range in people's willingness to forgive is as vast as the ever-growing list of gender identities.

Finally, Liz pulls up, twenty minutes late. She's wearing over-sized sunglasses and a baby blue scarf to protect her hair; she looks like she's starring in a film noir. Dorian opens the car door and surveys the passenger side floor, coated in a flotsam of Starbucks cups girdled in their cardboard sleeves, lipsticky napkins, empty Mountain Dew bottles. It's a discordancy about Liz: she's personally so stylish, yet the spaces she inhabits are so messy and gross. She's like a glossy, white guinea pig who shits everywhere in its cage. Dorian gingerly sits, kicking aside debris so she has a place to put her feet.

"So what the hell is a pre-engagement?" Liz says. "Is this like giving someone a promise ring?"

"God," Dorian says. "I didn't even consider that there might be a ring. With this ring, I promise that I will seriously consider committing to you?"

"There's a ring for everything these days. My creep-monster brother gave my niece one of those purity rings. You know, to symbolize that she should not give her body to some boy because she's daddy's little girl?" Liz says. "It's a wonder he didn't just brand her with a hot poker."

Dorian groans. She has met Liz's brother, whose shiny, pink face makes her think of boiled ham. The Labor Day barbecue where they were introduced, Stu kept glaring, as if Dorian would do something deviant were he to take his eyes off her.

"Did I ever tell you about that exhibition on chastity belts I saw at the Musée de Cluny, when Claudia and I took that trip to Paris?" When Liz shakes her head, Dorian says, "It was so bizarre. They were these bulky metal contraptions—I don't know why they're called belts. More like chastity Spanx. And they had these slits, I suppose so women wearing them could pee or bleed. But not holes big enough for a dick to fit into, of course. We stood there gaping at them, and then Claudia said, 'Those sure don't seem very sanitary.'"

Liz laughs, reminding Dorian of how she feels when her kindergartners and first-graders guffaw over the Tab and Mac story. Somehow, she can't adequately convey her horror. Not just at the chastity belts, but at Claudia's response to them: disgusted, but not for reasons Dorian understood. They'd gone to the Musée de Cluny so Claudia, who had a thing for unicorns, could see the famous tapestries, and those had unsettled Dorian too. The virgin's white hand resting on the unicorn's forelock looked dead. After the chastity belts, she'd felt sick, incapable of participating in the game she and Claudia played in museums, to keep from getting overwhelmed or bored: what was the thing in each room they would most like to own? When Claudia said, "Which chalice?" Dorian had said, "None of them," and then, "Let's get out of here."

Dorian removes the flask from her purse and takes a sip.

Liz says, "I thought you brought that for Claudia."

"I did, but I'm having second thoughts."

Liz is quiet. Dorian is pretty sure she knows what Liz is thinking: that second thoughts are why Claudia is getting pre-engaged to Tab instead of Dorian.

Second thoughts is a misnomer, at least in Dorian's case. Ideas don't pass through her brain in a single file line the way children exit the school library behind their teachers to return to their classrooms. In Dorian's head, thoughts move more like molecules in those molecular motion diagrams, zipping around in all directions—sometimes colliding, sometimes not.

At this particular moment, while Dorian is inundated with conflicting thoughts about Claudia, she is also wavering on whether or not she should get a haircut, whether that hawk flying overhead has a mouse or a lizard or something else in its talons, and whether or not spotting the hawk with its prey is some kind of omen. She knows this: Claudia would say that it is. But what Claudia would read into the hawk is difficult to predict, like when they stopped on a country road once for a family of skunks crossing, and Claudia announced that the skunks were an omen that they should not go to Guatemala, where Dorian wanted to go for vacation—hence Paris.

"Speaking of second thoughts," Dorian says, "How about we bail on this pre-engagement party, whatever the fuck that is? How about we go to Ocean Beach instead and watch the waves? It's a beautiful day."

Liz keeps driving, though Dorian bets she is tempted. "It's a beautiful day" was always the abracadabra incantation that worked on Liz, that back in college could induce her to bail on French History, Revolution to Fin de Siècle, and instead roll the tight joints that were her specialty. A talent that has outlived its use, like being a lady's milliner, or a maker of carriage wheels, but once made Liz not merely a beloved but also a useful friend.

"No, we should go to this," Liz decides, at last. "We don't need to stay long, but you need to make an appearance."

"Why?"

"Because if you go, you don't have to attend their wedding. You will have already proven yourself to be a good sport."

"Fuck being a good sport. Good sportsmanship is the most over-rated virtue on the planet! Seriously, Liz, good sportsmanship is what people with power use to blunt women's competitive instincts. 'Be a good sport, honey.' It's like a chastity belt for one's ambition."

"That makes zero sense."

Dorian feels like stamping her foot, but the floor is too littered with Starbucks cups. She thinks about the other day, telling one of her kindergartners, Trinity, to calm down and stop making a fuss. "But I need to make a fuss!" Trinity protested, and Dorian had thought, the kid is right: Sometimes you need to make a damn fuss. Not for the first time, she decided that children were emotionally smarter than most adults.

"You didn't want to marry Claudia, recall?" Liz says. "You thought she was shallow and kind of dumb. And Tab adores Claudia. And Tab's a good person. You haven't met them, Dorian. To be perfectly honest, I like them."

"Them," Dorian snorts. Liz has perfect brown and cream shoes with leather buttons, and perfect command of her pronouns, and Dorian is tempted to throw a Mountain Dew bottle at her.

"You can do this," Liz says. Though her comment, Dorian knows, is intended to be galvanizing—you can do this! Liz as a football captain, or Henry V, rallying his troops—Dorian hears her skepticism. Can she do this? That's debatable.

When they pull up to the house Claudia shares with Tab, and they can hear Edith Piaf singing "Je ne regrette rien" before they've even exited the car, Liz's skepticism manifests itself in her hands, which do not release their grip on the steering wheel. Then she says, "God, I'm sorry, Dorian. If you want me to drive away right now, I will. I'll take you to the beach or a bar, wherever you want."

Dorian wonders if the creature in the hawk's claws had still been alive, and if so, did it experience some awe at seeing the world from high above, taking in so much of it at once, for the first and only time in its life?

She says to Liz, "Fuck Claudia. We're going in. I want to see this Tab. I want to see this ring. I want to view the whole shit show."

A child in a rubber-ducky yellow pantsuit opens the door

when Dorian knocks. There's a half-eaten pink macaron in his free hand.

In Paris, Claudia was on a quest to find the best macaron. Every day she insisted on trying a different pâtisserie, and she posted pictures on Instagram of the various contenders. Dorian can't remember when or where or even if they had sex in Paris, but she remembers the winning macaron, two-toned like Liz's shoes, crème fraiche and lime. Dorian remembers standing on Rue Bonaparte, while Claudia waited in line at some overpriced pâtisserie, and wishing she were by herself in Guatemala.

The problem isn't, Dorian decides, second thoughts, which are merely returning to reality from some romantic acid trip. The problem is first thoughts: the way love makes one moronic and smitten, or, rather, moronic because smitten, and therefore, makes one ignore all the obvious issues (how can one form a long-term relationship with a former Tri Delt? With a woman who gets honey blonde highlights, so her hair is striated, like a ribeye steak? Who faithfully watches every season of *The Voice*?). Under first thought influence, one rashly promises forever, because en-cased in a post-orgasm stupor. Stupor and stupid: those words must share a root. To stoop, to demean oneself.

To say, after one's lover emerges from an eleventh pâtisserie with yet another damn macaron, "Hey, wait a minute, let's pause, let's reassess," isn't cruel or callous. It's evidence of maturity, of the higher brain asserting, albeit belatedly, like a spaced-out stu-dent at roll call, that it is Here after all.

THE CUCUMBER
IN THE OFFICE FRIDGE

MANAGEMENT HAS BEEN DIALING BACK THE thermostat since the company started losing money. Three years ago, I kept a red cardigan in my cubicle, which I took home every payday to wash and brought back to work the following Monday. Two years ago, the cardigan hung all summer on the plastic hook on my cubicle wall. I didn't wash it because I didn't wear it. One year ago, I bought a miniature electric fan for my desk. Now I have that fan set to the highest setting, and I'm still sweating. Instead of the cardigan, I keep deodorant in my cubicle, in the drawer with the butterfly clips, reserve staples, and sticky notes.

When I relay this to Ingrid, who has been here as long as I have, she says, "And don't forget about the fridge."

The intern, Molly, or as Ingrid and I call her, Cheap Labor, says, "What about the fridge?"

"We speculate that at any given moment, there are at least half a dozen rotten items in there." Ingrid frowns at the bits of olives and green peppers someone dumped in the kitchen sink.

"When we say rotten, we mean unrecognizable," I say.

On more than one occasion I've observed food so hairy it looked like a chia pet. I open the fridge now to show Molly the cucumber that has sat on the middle shelf for several weeks. Where a quarter of it has been sliced off, the skin has crumpled and curled around the edges of the now-spongy innards. It makes me think of an uncircumcised penis, only flatter.

We tell Molly there was a time when the fridge had been regularly cleaned. Every other month, we were directed to remove anything we wanted. Anything left over was tossed. Poof, clean fridge. The fridge had not been cleaned since I stopped wearing the cardigan.

"It's the tipping point," says Ingrid sagely, and tells us about some study of bathrooms in airplanes. Initially people clean up after themselves, throw away the rough paper for drying hands, flush the toilet. But once someone quits trying—leaves paper wadded up on the floor instead—everyone's like, Fuck it. "It's the broken window paradigm—you know, when people stop replacing windows, there goes the neighborhood. Here, we're all in this torpor. I mean, look at that fucking thing." We stare at the cucumber. There are little sinkholes where the seeds used to be, like they've gotten sucked into its mulchy interior, and the effect is creepy. It's like the cucumber has eye pits and is staring back.

"I guess being gross and lazy is better than stealing," says Molly, and tells us about her last job at a bar, where everyone helped themselves to the tip jar. "First it was just Rachel—everyone knew she was stealing. With my own eyes I saw her take a handful of bills. But she was sleeping with Rick, the guy who owned the bar, so no one had the balls to complain. Then eventually we were like, this sucks, and it was just a free for all. People grabbing money, not even bothering to hide it. Like what you said—" she nods at Ingrid. "Fuck it."

I feel a wave of sadness that's more than just crap job related. You could say the same about my home life. Hugh's gym socks on the floor, not even close to the hamper; the way he hogs the ottoman when we sit on the couch to watch TV. We used to put the ottoman in the middle and both have our feet on it, tangle our feet together. That was sometimes the start of something. Now the ottoman is always flush on his side. Now there are designated sides to the couch.

An hour later, Ingrid emails me a link to an article: "Ten Signs Your Workplace is Toxic." Although nothing on that list is new to me—Ingrid and I have complained about every one of those things over the years, from management playing favorites to the promises they don't keep to the ridiculous ways they micromanage, specifying the number of inches our computer monitors should be from our eyes and that we shouldn't leave from the back of the building because there is no sidewalk and we could lose our footing in the dirt (everyone knows the real reason is that management can't monitor our coming and going from the back of the building, given that their offices are up front)—somehow seeing all the shit we put up with organized into a checklist that confirms a diagnosis, makes me woozy.

Ingrid DMs me, "God, if this were a romantic relationship, no way would I have stuck around this long. What's wrong with us?"

Not that I'd call my home life "toxic." Toxic means poisonous. Toxic is that cucumber that is puffing out spores of death. Toxic is the coating of dust on the exhaust fan in the women's bathroom.

But.

Ingrid writes, "Well, the pay is good. That's why I stick around."

I look out my office window at the tent and sleeping bags a couple of unhoused people people set up in the thin strip of land between our building and the property next door. They've been here nearly three months—a woman with long brown hair, a guy who's clean-shaven despite living outdoors. Management can't do anything about them because technically they're on public land. Sometimes as they pass by my window, they look at me. I always wonder what they're thinking. Do they envy me? Do they pity me?

I wonder what they would say to our complaints about rotting food and dust and air conditioning. What they would say about Hugh's feet monopolizing the ottoman. About the way I monitor the quality of my space, the way my energy goes into resenting that damn cucumber, rather than tossing it.

TO BE GENEROUS

When Amy whispered in Russ's ear that what he wanted would cost him fifty bucks, she meant it to be sexy. She imagined him slapping a bill down on the nightstand, next to the philosophy textbook she'd been muddling through in an effort to better endure conversation with the other mothers chaperoning tomorrow night's eighth-grade dance. She imagined Russ tying her wrists to the bedpost the way he used to do before they had the kids, before they had the house—only an apartment with walls so thin their neighbors' pot smoke seemed to pass through them by osmosis. In those days it hadn't mattered that they were broke, because sex was free entertainment. Nor had it mattered that Amy was loud in bed: it was appropriate retaliation for the neighbors' incessant Grateful Dead. Though sometimes Amy had felt fidgety when she passed Charley and Rhodes in the hallway, swinging their pungent take-out bags. Even with her eyes downcast, Amy could feel them exchanging a snickering glance, telepathing, "There goes The Moaner."

But Russ just said, "My money is our money. That'd be like me buying groceries and calling it a gift to you."

"Groceries?" Amy said. "A gift to *me*?"

From above her, where he kneeled next to her face, Russ grinned.

Amy sat up. "My money is our money too. And for the record: buying groceries *is* a gift. Of time. Between the list-making and the driving and the shopping and the putting things away, I probably spend four or more hours a week offering you and the kids the gift of groceries."

Now Russ fished his briefs from under the sheets and pulled them back on. Because she'd referenced the kids.

Russ contended that mentioning the kids during sex was akin to loudly announcing to deer that you've come to hunt them. You might as well forget about killing any deer. Amy had always found this metaphor puzzling. For one, Russ had never hunted. He didn't even fish. Two, what represented what in this metaphor? Was his erection the deer? And who was the gun? Ludicrous to imagine sweet, brown-eyed Oscar in the role: eight years old, yet still sleeping with the stuffed rabbit he'd won at a carnival when he was four. Or Vera, either: always with her head in a book, that one. Daphne, their middle child, was a better fit: there was something fierce and smoking about her. Amy knew from her friend Elise that one of the other moms, Rachel McKay, had recently called Daphne a bully.

Amy watched Russ pull on his T-shirt and considered the expression, "holding one's tongue." The list of things to not say during sex had grown ridiculous. Russ could vocalize any banal sentiment that came to mind, and Amy had to not object to his paucity of diction: wet, hard, turned on. Surely someone college educated could be more original? Whereas she had to tread cautiously. It was like when her mother had made soufflés: tiptoeing around the kitchen, softly closing the fridge, because any moderate noise could deflate the thing.

God forbid Amy mention the thoughts drifting through her head when they fooled around, not just the internal wincing at Russ's hackneyed sex talk, but also the mental sticky notes she would write herself: hardware store tomorrow to buy the special lightbulbs for the bubble chandelier. Thaw chicken for dinner. Russ was like an exotic orchid that would only flourish under optimal conditions, a flower that required a heat lamp and spritzing from an atomizer.

———

In the kitchen the next morning, Daphne was saying to Oscar, "There's no such thing as a soul. The brain and the body are just a machine."

"Like a computer?" Oscar said. He poked the pastry tart on his plate and then jerked his finger back again. Too hot.

"More a computer is like a brain," Daphne said. "Only not as interesting because computers have to be programmed. Of course, brains can be programmed too. Like when people raise their kids to believe in things like souls and gods, instead of just letting them think for themselves."

This conversation told Amy that Russ was either out running or Daphne was looking for trouble. Russ never pressed religion on the kids. He wasn't the evangelical type, nor would Amy stand for preachiness. But he got prickly when Daphne spoke dismissively of religion or anything else he cared about, namely football and the summer sausage at Dick's Delicatessen.

Amy was relieved when Russ appeared in the T-shirt he'd slept in—not because this proved that Daphne was trying to rile him up, but because Amy felt excused from the burden of getting exercise herself.

"I wonder where she got that from," he said to Amy as he poured coffee into her I-Figuratively-Die-As-I-Hear-You-Literally-Abuse-Words mug.

When Amy answered that the apple doesn't fall far from the tree, Russ fired back, "Where's my damn apple? Three kids and they're all your apples?"

Oscar said, "But Daddy, you don't like apples."

"No one likes apples," Daphne said. "Apples suck. That's why it makes no sense for Eve to get herself and Adam kicked out of Eden for an apple! At least make breaking the rules something worth mortality and pain in childbirth forevermore. Though who knew God would fly off the handle like that? I mean, over-reaction much?"

All three of the humans who were not Russ, Daphne in particular, flicked their eyes his way, to see how Russ would take this pronouncement. Russ blinked, then said, "I told you not to say 'suck.'"

Amy's thought, fleeting and disloyal, was what a hypocrite her husband was: he'd used that verb the night before, admittedly applying it in a literal sense.

Daphne waved dismissively. "Mr. Benn says fruit is a symbol for temptation in all those old myths." Again, everyone's eyes cast to Russ, to see how he would respond to this application of "myth."

"Take poor Persephone. She gets stuck in the Underworld for six months out of the year, and you know why? For the great, great crime of eating six seeds of pomegranate while Hades kept her captive! At least pomegranates taste good; at least they're not a completely lame fruit, like apples. But doesn't six months in the Underworld for all eternity for eating six seeds seem a trifle excessive? I guess in the olden days, people didn't have much else available to represent temptation."

Daphne contemplated the uneaten half of an Old-Fashioned donut in her hand, then looked wonderingly at Amy, who wasn't sure how to interpret the look. Did Daphne want confirmation of her insight about symbolism? It was one way Amy bonded with her middle child, listening to Daphne spin theories about song lyrics, the president's tweets, the rotten state of the world. Or was Amy supposed to be some kind of native informant from the Olden Days herself? Amy resisted the urge to curtsey, or to say "Milady." Instead, she changed the subject to the dance.

"I've changed my mind about not caring if you sit this one out," she said to Russ. "I want you to be my date."

Russ squinted at her over the rim of her coffee mug.

"When's the last time we danced together?"

Russ said, "You make fun of my dancing."

"Because you have no rhythm," Daphne said before Amy could.

"I feel like I'm moving to the beat." He opened the pantry and closed it, opened the refrigerator and closed it, went back to the pantry again. "Is there nothing to eat in this house?"

Amy said, "You're so off the beat sometimes, it's like you're dancing to a completely different genre of music." She stared at the back of his head from where he stood before the pantry, willing him to surprise her with a dip or spin. But when he did turn, he gave her a look like she'd just shoved him, and now he was deciding whether to hit her back or to walk away.

He said, "I'm not going to that dance."

Oscar pointed to the box of pastry tarts. His mouth full, he mumbled, "There's food."

Vera returned from spending the night at her friend Samantha's house while Amy was making a grocery list. Amy could swear she smelled the cat on Vera whenever she returned from Samantha's. That girl's family had eight cats, and when Vera slept over there, the cats piled around her sleeping bag and her face. As soon as Vera closed the door, her hand went to her tongue, no doubt removing a feline hair. Then she said, "FYI: the trees are wrapped."

"Knox!" Daphne said. She dropped her phone and ran outside.

"Not again," Amy said. This prank-off between Daphne and fellow eighth-grader Eli Knox had taken Hatfield and McCoy proportions. It was one thing when the pranks merely affected the two participants. Then they had been charming. Amy had particularly admired the one where Eli had used a fine-point pen to draw X's on the eyes of Daphne's animal crackers, rendering them all unconscious or dead. But, of course, it was the nature of feuds to spin out of control, to suck into their vortex hapless innocents. Last week Bryn Knox had sent Amy a jpeg of all the Knox garden gnomes walking the plank—the plank being a two-by-four extending from the Knox's treehouse, over which hung a paper banner depicting a skull and bones. Amy had found that funny, too, though Bryn had not been amused—one of the girl gnomes had fallen into a flower bed. A second photo Bryn sent had documented her shattered bosom.

"Why can't kids flirt with each other like we all did?" Amy said to Russ, who was looking out the kitchen window, assessing the damage.

"All I know is I'm not cleaning up any of that toilet paper," he said darkly.

She wasn't sure what generated his grumpiness—if this was about the dance moves, or about last night. But Amy regretted the timing. All week she had been stressing about this eighth-grade dance. Elise, Amy's only real friend amongst the parents at Daphne's school, her dearest friend in town, in fact, wouldn't be there because she had enough shit on her plate lately with her husband's early onset Parkinson's. Not to mention she and Jonathan had twin five-year-old boys. When she was in one of her better moods, Elise joked that Jonathon's various extracurricular activities—swimming, climbing, cycling, and boxing; exercise was one of the few things proven to help maintain some mobility as the disease symptoms progressed—competed with her four kids' activities combined.

Rachel McKay labeling Daphne a bully was not something Amy could will away. As for brushing up on Socratic reasoning, what had begun as an earnest effort to remind herself to question her assumptions and to be more open to alternative viewpoints had devolved into a stockpiling of arms. Amy pictured her questions like fiery cannonballs blasting Rachel McKay into the gymnasium's walls: *Did you know that your precious Lana nicknamed Daphne "Bleeder" because of her heavy periods? Who's the fucking bully now, Rachel?*

So much for the artful establishment of common ground.

If only Russ would come! Russ was so much more genial. There was an inverse correlation between quality of talk and his aptitude: Russ improved with each downward gradation, excelling at the smallest of talk.

Also, Amy felt particularly close to Russ when it was the two of them together versus some external, hostile force. In their own house, he could sometimes seem like the enemy. But outside, they were a team, and a damn good one. When their neighbor came home with a dog and then left the poor thing chained up in the backyard all day and night, where it barked at all hours, she and Russ had taken turns blowing a dog whistle. When that didn't work, Russ had climbed a ladder at midnight to rig up an ultrasonic device under the cover of darkness. Amy had held the ladder, handed him pieces of duct tape.

She slipped her arms around him from behind and pressed her cheek against his back. Russ remained rigid, though. When he acted like this, she always thought of the biggest fight they'd ever had, which had been over her getting an abortion when she ended up pregnant unexpectedly. Oscar hadn't even been two yet. He'd still been nursing. A third child had been harder than she'd anticipated—starting all over again when Daphne had finally begun kindergarten. She'd worried for her mental and physical health if she carried that baby to term.

"If you'll come to this dance with me, I'll be in your debt. Anything you want," Amy said. She reached a hand up under his shirt and caressed the hairs on his abdomen.

"What I want is that toilet paper cleaned up before it rains," he said.

She followed his gaze to where dark clouds had gathered.

"You're on," she said and booked out to the front yard before Russ could respond.

—

Removing the toilet paper from their three trees, which Eli had wrapped so meticulously that they looked like powder puffs, reminded Amy of taking down the Christmas tree. Decorating the tree was always festive, the family all in it together. The kids would erupt in squeals when they unpacked from bubble wrap their particular special ornaments. For Daphne, it was the little girl with red braids and three freckles on each cheek, the girl who had been Amy's own special ornament when she was a kid. Taking down the tree, however, was another story. Amy was on her own then: no one wanted to help with that depressing chore. Little could make Amy feel quite so sorry for herself, so burdened with every repellent task, than taping the little girl with the braids back in bubble wrap, sweeping up the dead pine needles, untangling the stringed lights.

And the toilet paper was more a pain in the ass than the

Christmas lights, because it was so fragile: it kept tearing as Amy yanked it down. The only procedure that worked, she discovered, was to hold one end gently and walk around and around the tree, looping the paper over her hands so it looked like she was wearing white boxing gloves. She tried to feel Zen about revolving in endless circles. Hey, she was getting exercise after all!

Oscar had asked her recently what superpower she'd choose if she could have any superpower she wanted, and Amy had said the power to complete chores at the snap of her fingers, like Mary Poppins. Oscar had looked disappointed, said she wasn't taking his question seriously, but, of course, she'd been dead serious. She'd said that if he had to do half as many chores as she did, he'd think her choice both desirable and astute. He'd shrugged and left her to finish scrubbing the toilet.

Daphne, assigned to the tallest tree, made slower progress. "Knox is fucking dead," she kept saying. But Daphne sounded more energized than angry. Like Russ when they were housesitting years ago and he cheered on their friend's cat Starfucker as it cornered a trembling mouse beneath the friend's wine cabinet.

By the time they were pulling the last of the toilet paper from the top branches, Daphne wedged in the fork of the ornamental plum tree, the rain started splashing down. Amy's paper boxing gloves transformed into a clumpy mess, like plaster. She felt as though she'd barely dodged a catastrophe. Like the time she almost hit a pedestrian crossing the street. The elderly woman had been perfectly concealed by the strip of metal between the car's front window and the driver's side window. That, and Amy had been flustered by construction delays—Oscar sure to be tardy at school yet again. The woman's eyes had widened as Amy slammed on the brakes. Amy wondered still: if she had hit the woman and there'd been any way she might get away with lying about how it had happened, would she have? She'd lied to Oscar that morning, claimed the woman had not been paying attention. She'd used the incident as an opportunity to remind him to be cautious when crossing streets.

———

Amy called Elise on the way to the grocery store to find out if she needed anything. Elise didn't live particularly close, but Amy was sensitive about being a good friend to Elise. They'd known each other since their oldest children were newborns, born on the same day in the same small birthing center. Amy had labored over night, given birth to Vera early on a Friday morning. When a few hours later she'd heard a woman screaming bloody murder down the hallway, she'd laughed out loud, even though the laughter had been painful. Difficult to explain to Russ why the woman's screaming was funny, so soon after she'd been screaming like that, but it was. Amy loved the woman right then and there. When they finally met at the birth center's mom-and-baby group they'd bonded with a fierceness Amy hadn't experienced since high school.

"I'm not going to lie," Elise said, "I could really use a fucking slice of cheesecake right now."

"I'm bringing you a whole cheesecake," Amy said. "Chocolate?"

Elise said, "No, no. I'm just kidding." Then, "Actually, I'm not kidding."

The hard thing, or maybe the good thing, depending on how you looked at it, about having a friend in Elise's particular situation is that it wasn't as easy to feel sorry for yourself. Amy had once read a Stanford study that concluded people's contentment was not based on the real circumstances of their lives, but how well they measured up against their peer group. Subjects of the study reported feeling "poor" when their friends were better off, despite their lack of debt, or all their material goods; other subjects, with lower income levels, but less affluent peers, reported feeling "well off" or "lucky." Happiness was relative.

Though forty-five minutes later, sitting in Elise's kitchen, the two of them forking up giant wedges of cheesecake, Amy felt less satisfied with her own relative comfort. Elise poured them each a glass of milk, and drinking it, Amy couldn't help comparing now to back when Vera and Owen were babies. Then it was mimosas, not calcium-fortified milk, and Elise poured the champagne with a free hand. Vera and Owen rolled around on the exercise mat, while their mothers played desultory games of Scrabble—one baby usually cut short the game by needing a nap—got tipsy, and gossiped about the most annoying mother in the mom's group, the one who bragged about her son's developmental skills under the guise of asking questions. "Are your babies crawling yet?" When Amy was on her own, this woman made Amy feel awful, worried that Vera was developmentally delayed, and that these delays, though seemingly small, represented more than Amy could see, the way that a centimeter on a map might be equal to a hundred miles in the real world. But Elise, like the champagne, fortified Amy. Then the mother became mockable.

"Damn, Elise, I wish you were going to that dance tonight. I need you."

In the living room, the twins yelled, "Take that!" "No, take that!" They were sword fighting with cardboard wrapping-paper rolls.

"Believe me, I wish I could. But you'll have Russ."

Amy registered everything underneath the two statements. Jonathon's medication conked him out. He was half asleep by dinner, snoring by 8 p.m. many nights, leaving Elise to put the twins to bed. Was Elise pissed at her, or was she just imagining it? Could anyone resent a friend who brought them cheesecake? She wanted to press Elise for details about what exactly Rachel McKay said about Daphne. Elise had been weirdly vague the other day, reluctant, volunteering only, "Daphne said something obnoxious. Something about Lana being ugly." When Amy had said, "That's ridiculous!" Elise had gone silent, and soon after said she had to go because one of the twins had gotten out of bed and was complaining of growing pains. Only later, replaying their conversation, did Amy realize Elise had reported, "Daphne said." Not "Daphne allegedly said."

"Hey, do you remember that weird, braggy mom from moms' group? You called her Ms. Fine Motor Skills?"

Elise looked blank, then said, "Oh yeah. Stephanie, right?" She tilted her face, quizzical. "What made you think of her?"

When Amy didn't answer, Elise pressed the back of her fork onto the spongy top of her cheesecake slice, then turned it sideways and pressed it again. The crosshatch looked like griddle marks on a steak.

***

It was nearly four by the time Amy got home from the grocery store. She had to be at the school gymnasium by half past five to report for duty. That gave her little over an hour to put away the groceries, feed herself and her family something quick and easy (for that, she'd picked up deli meats and sliced cheeses), shower, and get dressed. No sweat, assuming Russ was cooperative. But when the garage door retracted to reveal Russ, still unshaven, punching the punching bag, Amy took a deep breath.

"Just so you know, we need to leave in fifty-five minutes," she said, stripping off fifteen minutes. Russ was always running late, even for events he wanted to attend. Because he was always misplacing things—most commonly, his wallet (which unnerved Amy to no end), but also his car keys, his phone, his belt, his razor, you name it. To make matters worse, he became crazed when frantically searching for some lost item. He tore through the house like The Hulk, obliterating anything or anyone who got in his way.

"Got it," Russ said.

Amy hesitated. "You're planning to shower and shave, right?"

"Plenty of time," Russ said.

"Can you maybe do it while I put the groceries away and make sandwiches?"

"What's the worst that can happen?" he said. "If I'm not ready in time, you can always just go without me."

"That's not funny," she said.

Russ winked at her. Then he punched the bag so hard she flinched. She considered sprinkling powdered laxatives into the mustard of his sandwich.

Inside, Daphne and Oscar were watching a shark documentary, Daphne painting her fingernails black. Amy was relieved that Daphne's hair was wet, that they wouldn't all three be competing to shower at once. Also, she was impressed at how breezy Daphne was, sitting there in T-shirt and shorts, watching sharks rip apart prey, instead of anxiously primping in front of a mirror. Vera wasn't a primper either, but that was different, because Vera didn't even go to her eighth-grade dance. At Daphne's age, Amy hadn't had a fraction of her confidence. If she could recover the hours she spent messing with her hair and her skin back then, she could probably write a fucking book or learn a foreign language.

Of course, that premise assumed Amy would use her salvaged time productively, instead of, say, the way this day had gone: unspooling toilet paper from trees, checking the expiration dates on packages of bacon, searching for Russ's high-protein chocolate pea milk, surreptitiously squeezing mangoes because Vera would only eat unripe ones, flesh barely yellow, so unripe that when Vera bit into them, they crunched. In fifth grade, Amy's math teacher, reviewing long multiplication, had once casually announced to her class that the average person, dying at age 80, lived 29,200 days. That number had horrified Amy and stuck with her ever since, a mote she couldn't quite get out of her eye.

Time may be habitually wasted, but it also rushed by much too quickly. Amy, taking too long to figure out what to wear, never had a chance to eat one of the sandwiches she'd made, so at the dance hovered over the refreshment table, nibbling her third frosted sugar cookie. The cookie didn't even taste good. It had no nuance. It reduced itself to one-word adjectives: "sweet," "crunchy." Elise called food like this, food that supplied no pleasure, which one ate purely because of biological imperative, "food product."

Russ, despite his endless complaints, looked perfectly content, leaning against the wall talking to Paul Hoberman. Those two were probably dissecting the Dallas Cowboys; it was a topic Russ could go on and on about. "Conversation product."

The gymnasium was decorated with columns of silver and seafoam green balloons. "Under the Sea" was the theme. More like "In a Vernal Pool," Amy thought.

Before her field of vision sprinted a boy in a thrift-store jacket with large silver buttons. Amy admired the jacket before she processed the kid's face, and when she did, she pointed, and said more loudly than she intended, "Eli Knox! You're so dead."

Eli Knox looked at Amy as one might a never-before-seen species of animal through the safety of a thick pane of glass. Neither fear nor remorse showed on his face, just curiosity. He had no idea what she was talking about. The expression on Rachel McKay's face, on the other hand—she looked up in the midst of refilling the punch bowl—was unmistakably judgy. "It's no mystery where Daphne gets it from," Amy imagined Rachel saying to a group of the other mothers. She pictured Elise in that coterie too, serving up slices of the cheesecake Amy had brought her. (And mimosas!) "Did I tell you all about the time Amy scared off some woman from her yoga class who was interested in the house up for sale next door to her? Made up shit about pack rats and scorpions, just because she didn't want this woman living so close to her," Amy imagined Elise saying.

"You had nothing to do with the toilet paper that mummi-fied our trees this morning?" Amy said to Knox, lowering her voice.

"Honestly, I didn't," he said. "I told Daphne already. I mean, she does have it coming, you have to admit. But that wasn't me."

"She has it coming?" Amy glanced at Rachel McKay.

"That was my mom's favorite gnome," Knox said. "Her best friend gave it to her. I had to hear all about it."

Amy scanned the room until she spotted Daphne on the dance floor in her stunningly simple black dress. Many of the other girls looked like overpriced candies in their fuchsias and sapphire blues and emerald greens, their dresses adorned with tulle and lace and sequins. Amy remembered her own eighth-grade dance, how her hair had been stiff as meringue with all that hairspray, her dress pink and glittery, like something out of Cirque du Soleil. In contrast, Daphne reminded Amy of Melanie Pierce, the girl who had always seemed effortlessly beautiful. God, how Amy had hated Melanie Pierce. Had Melanie ever done or said anything mean to Amy? Honestly, Amy couldn't remember, only that Melanie's very existence had felt like an assault. It was that Stanford study again, contentment measured in compari-son to one's peers: Melanie Pierce was the benchmark that made Amy gawky, shaggy, pathetic.

"But if you didn't toilet paper the yard..." said Amy.

"No clue," said Knox. "You know Daph: it could be anyone."

Amy watched him meander toward the black dress on the dance floor. Her daughter, a thirteen-year-old mash-up of Audrey Hepburn and the Godfather, surrounded by scheming enemies with toilet paper rolls in their holsters.

She studied Rachel McKay, who was stirring the punch so aggressively orange slices whirled in a gyre. Rachel McKay looked up, and the two women exchanged a glance that dispensed with various pretenses.

"Oh, come on," Rachel McKay said. "I'm an adult. I didn't toilet-paper your frigging lawn."

"Then—" said Amy.

"You heard that kid! 'It could be anyone.' Sounds like your daughter isn't particularly popular."

Though they both knew that the opposite was true: Daphne was popular, as Melanie Pierce had been popular, and popularity begat its own venom. Amy suddenly knew, or rather recognized something she had subconsciously always known, that Melanie Pierce had never done anything mean to her, ever. No doubt Melanie Pierce would be confounded to learn that forty-four-year-old Amy (if she even remembered Amy) was still obsessing about her.

All pointers from Socrates fled Amy's brain. Rachel McKay's round, white face reminded her of the dim sum she and Elise used to order at Shanghai Palace—the puffy pork buns. The McKays had moved from Arkansas just last August, and Amy had only seen Rachel McKay in person two or three times. She was far more familiar with her Facebook profile picture. Rachel McKay had ignored Amy's one Friend request, lobbed at her several days ago, but she was Friends with Elise. In the profile picture, Rachel McKay was in Halloween costume as Princess Leah, the giant Cinnabon buns of hair competing with the roundness of her face. She looked much less ridiculous in person.

"Why are you so anti Daphne?" Amy said, at last.

Rachel McKay looked taken aback, then unhappy. Two vertical pleats appeared around her mouth. "Your daughter called my daughter a dog," she said at last.

Amy followed Rachel McKay's eyes to the girl talking to the DJ. She was barefoot, a pair of red kitten heels dangling from her hand, yet still taller than most of the kids in the room. She had a head of beautiful, curly, brown hair.

"That's your daughter?" Amy asked.

"Lana," Rachel said.

"Okay, one, I'm confident Daphne wouldn't call another girl a dog, and two, there's no way she would call your daughter a dog. She's gorgeous!"

"Lana heard her," Rachel said.

Amy understood there was much she would never know about her children, or Russ, for that matter. She accepted that fact, even appreciated it. How boring if people were static and transparent—no mystery, no nuance, no surprises. She thought of the sheet that always came with furniture you had to build yourself: "Before beginning to assemble, make sure the following items are included in the package. If anything is missing, contact the retailer."

When Elise had first told Amy about Jonathan's early onset Parkinson's, Elise said she felt betrayed, as though she'd discovered Jonathan had cheated on her or depleted their 401K account or, heck, murdered somebody. "I know that's a completely unfair analogy," she'd said, "that Parkinson's isn't a secret he was keeping from me, but already, it's like he's a different person. And it's going to get so much worse."

"Listen, I'm not naïve about my kids," Amy said now to Rachel McKay. "I know they can be heinous. But the thing about that comment—Daphne would be politically opposed to it. She would consider it misogynist." Rachel McKay stared back at her, unconvinced, biting her bottom lip. She seemed to be in the process of eating her own mouth. It was a weird, startling image that reminded Amy of an ouroboros, the snake that consumed its own tail. As if this image shook something loose, Amy said, "Wait. Is Lana the girl who's always scratching?"

The question made Rachel McKay eject her lips, restored her face into its prior expression of righteous indignation. "What!?"

"She has some kind of rash on her arms? What I mean is, is it possible that Daphne said Lana was 'like a dog,' meaning she scratches herself like a dog, and what Lana heard was, she merely was 'a dog'?"

"I don't get the distinction," Rachel McKay said, but then stopped, and in that unfolding pause Amy felt like an oracle, channeling Socrates himself. Skewering opponents was not Socrates's mode. He wanted to get the naysayers on his side. His remarks to them were not points scored; they were invitations to consensus, one his opponents couldn't see coming, admittedly, but that Socrates, always with the long view, spotted on the horizon. To be generous! Russ had that facility. "Honey, everyone screws up," he'd said to her, when Amy told him, in the middle of the night, about the old lady she had almost run over.

She waited for Rachel to look her in the eyes, and then began, in her most cajoling voice, to reassemble her evidence: their own beloved dog Meteor, dead two years, constantly clawing himself, because he had a skin condition; Daphne's aversion to all misogynistic rhetoric—her debate topic for Humanities, that she had to get special permission from Mr. Benn to broach given its controversial subject matter, was on the problematic word "bitch"; and finally, the objective reality of Lana, standing fifty feet away, radiating beauty like a sprinkler dispensing arcs of water. "I mean, come on, look at her," Amy finished. "Your daughter is hot!"

Rachel McKay shook her head. "That's a weird and inappropriate thing to say." But Amy saw that Rachel McKay was fighting a smile, and she did her damnedest to conceal her own.

Amy found Russ on the other side of the double doors connecting the gymnasium to the rest of the school. He was staring down the long hallway lined with blue metal lockers. Before he turned to look at her, she snaked her arms around his waist and pressed her nose against his back. He covered her hands with his own. Neither of them said anything for some time. Something about that space—maybe the familiarity of it, maybe the uniformity of the landscape, and maybe too that each locker was occupied temporarily by one individual but over time by dozens of students—made Amy feel as though she and Russ were on some kind of spacecraft, traveling high above Earth's surface. That reminded her—she still needed to replace the piece of luggage that had lost a wheel on her last flight.

Russ said, "This is nice, but I think I should tell you that I'm a married man."

"That's too bad," Amy said.

"Seventeen years now," Russ said.

"That's a long fucking time," Amy said.

She'd read in a magazine once that a good test of whether a troubled relationship could be mended rested in the couple's ability, and willingness, to remember the early days of their relationship, to see their partner again as they had long ago. She remembered saying to Russ, "Isn't that sort of like looking at a half-eaten and browning apple—or maybe even a shriveled, rotten core—and seeing it whole and ripe again? Isn't that just delusion?"

Now she said, "Did you toilet-paper my house last night?"

"You got me," Russ said.

"I'm going to have to get you back now, Russell Monson."

"Oh yeah? How?"

"I can't tell you that," Amy said.

Russ squeezed her thighs. "I'm starving," he said.

"Me too. All I had for dinner was three terribly subpar sugar cookies. And lunch was cheesecake!"

"Those cookies were bad," he said.

"They were a sad imitation of sugar cookies, like AstroTurf is to real grass. Like cookies a robot would make."

Russ said, "I saw you talking to what's-her-name for a long time. What were you talking about?"

"You mean Rachel McKay? A lot of things. I told her about condiment cake. It's some new crazy trend: mustard cake with ketchup frosting. Or maybe I have that reversed. Maybe it's ketchup cake with mustard frosting."

"Disgusting!"

Amy reflected, then said, "Agreed." Sometimes things just were what they were, and the literal adjective—wet, hard, sweet, disgusting—encapsulated them just fine.

PUBLICATIONS
FROM THIS COLLECTION

"Kindness Woman" *Cleaver* (September 17, 2019)

"Picking" *Heavy Feather Review* Volume 9 (2019)

"Oh-Oh-It's-Cruel" *Moon City Review* (2021)

"Accountability Buddies" *New World Writing*
(May 27, 2020)

"War" *Monkeybicycle* (August 11, 2017)

"Airship" *Pithead Chapel* (April 1, 2018)

"Amuse-bouches" *Split Lip Magazine* (September 2018)

"Rule of Thumb" *Notre Dame Review* Number 49
(Winter/Spring 2020)

"My Coworker Aldona" *(b)OINK* Issue 7 (September 2017)

"It Was Stapled to the Chicken" *Pinball*
(January 22, 2018)

"The Present Moment" *Okay Donkey* (August 2, 2019)

"Counterbalances" *Superstition Review* Issue 20
(Fall 2017)

"Twenty-three Safety Manuals" *Colorado Review* Volume 48
Number 1 (Spring 2021)

"Family Reunion: Inventories" *MoonPark Review*

(March 20, 2018)

"Disagree to Disagree" *Literary Mama* (January 21, 2019)

"Sun Spots" *Fictive Dream* (September 24, 2021)

"Night Vision" *Cleaver* Issue 34 (June 2021)

"Common Mistakes" *Superstition Review* (December 1, 2023)

"Spores" *Barren Magazine* Issue 10 (July 29, 2019)

"Deluxe Scrabble" *Cutleaf* (May 12, 2022)

"A Test I Knew I Could Pass" *Cagibi* (April 14, 2018)

"Abuse and Other Words My Mother and I Disagree About" *New World Writing* (July 17, 2019)

"Tab Is Sad" *Gravel* (November 2018)

"The Cucumber in the Office Fridge" *Fictive Dream* (March 6, 2020)

"To Be Generous" *Berkeley Fiction Review* Issue 39 (2019)

www.ingramcontent.com/pod-product-compliance
Lightning Source LLC
Chambersburg PA
CBHW061806190726
48289CB00007B/2090